THE PIPES ARE CALLING

A novel by Gabriel McNeil

for Ken with best wishes

from Gabriel

CHAPTER 1

"In Derry vale, beside the singing river,

So oft I strayed a many years ago"

"What's your name?" A man's voice.

"Where do you come from?" A different man.
"What's your name?"
"Where do you come from?"
These two questions were repeating over and over as if on a loop as I lay face down on a hard surface and men pummelled my back.
I knew my name. It was Grainne.

Or was it Geraldine? I struggled with that, trying to make some connections.
Suddenly I was heaved over onto my back.
"Where do you come from?" Said a huge mouth descending towards mine. Other mouths were moving in on me too. I screamed but nothing came out.

I came from Ireland, but these were not Irish voices. I wanted to ask them where I was. But nothing came out.
The mouth locked on mine and a huge breath forced itself into my lungs. I saw his eyes, big and staring like the wolf's in Red Ridinghood. The mouth drew away and other, horrible disembodied eyes hovered over me. More mouths opened.
"What's your name?"
"Where do you come from?"

I tried to tell them. Made a huge effort to move my mouth but it wouldn't work.

3

"Is she going to make it?
The mouth locked on mine again. Air forced itself into my body. The mouth withdrew.
  "Touch and go."
  "Brought her up by the feet. If I hadn't got her on the first dive she'd definitely be a gonner."
I heard a siren wail. Then nothing.

A novice swimmer, already struggling in the deep end when kids started screaming and jumping from the springboard, landing all around with huge competitive splashes, somebody bombed me on the way down and forced me underwater. But nobody noticed or cared. The water was churning and seething like a giant witch's cauldron and I was gasping and choking and drowning as the play went on indifferently all around. Like Icarus I drifted down, down, down to my death while children played and the world went about its business.

This had all happened before. The twins had launched me into Wylie's pond when I was only six to verify their theory that every creature was born with the ability to swim. To them I was a rather annoying and expendable little creature whom they had to drag along on their secret adventures. I remembered the terror and powerlessness and the suffocating feeling of water forcing its way into every orifice. My lungs were bursting with pain when suddenly I was dragged into the air and it rushed down my throat like the breath of life into Eve.

Pat Malloy had staggered out of Wylie's pond with me in his arms and unleashed a torrent of oaths at my sisters who were twice his age.
  "You pair of bitches," he shouted. "Just wait till I tell your ma about this!"

4

I fell to the ground as Maryanne grabbed him by the scruff of the neck and shook him as a terrier shakes a rat.

"Tell and you're for it, you skinny wee shite."

Struggling free, Pat pulled me up by the hand and ran off with me in tow, hurling abuse over his shoulder. That was the beginning of my lifelong bond with Pat Molloy. Together over the years we had many adventures until they were brought to an abrupt end when my family left Ireland.

Now I was lying in a hospital bed in Scotland, remembering the past and trying to make sense of the present. Suddenly it came back topsy-turvy in a terrible rush. My father would kill me when I got home for conning my way into a naval personnel swimming pool. He would see it as a wilful act of disobedience aimed at embarrassing him, the new MOD inspector of police, a position already resented by some of his men. Was there not a good enough man in Scotland for the job when they had to bring in this outsider from Northern Ireland? My father had brought this unspoken question with him to his new post.

Our father who is not in heaven, if there is one or if there is any justice in this world or hereafter. Our father who pulled us from our beds and slapped us warm if we complained about the cold in a bedroom where even the mice behind the skirting boards shivered. Our father who slipped his hands down nighties and felt our racing little hearts if we even as much as coughed in bed, before pronouncing us dirty little bitches. Our father, the giant at the top of the beanstalk, always threatening to destroy our world.

"God let me be ill enough to spend months in hospital," I prayed.

Then I wouldn't have to go back home to face him. I wouldn't have to go back to school. I wouldn't have to face the daily name-calling,

"Peasant! Peasant! Revolting Irish peasant!"

I had been dragged from my home and culture at an unfortunate time. My classmates in Scotland had already settled their friendships and seating arrangements by the time I joined my new high school in the middle of second year and my funny accent and lack of fashion made me the perfect target for ridicule. To be fair, I had drawn much of it on myself. That first day at school they nicknamed me "the Irish peasant" and thereafter it was impossible for anyone to become friends with me without incurring ridicule.

I had started off on the wrong foot because my very first class was history and it was just my luck that they were studying the Irish Question when I arrived for my first lesson and the class was bored with it. Seeing that I was new, the teacher turned to the class and said,

"I see we have a stranger in our midst," and asked me my name.

"Grainne, Grainne Kelly, Sir."

"Ah! Irish. How appropriate. How do you spell it?"

"G r a i n n e, sir."

"Are you a fugitive from the Troubles?"

He said this as he was adding my name to the class register. I wasn't sure how to take him and said nothing.

"Well, are you?" Have you got a tongue in your head?"

"I don't really know, Sir."

"Well if you don't, who does? No wonder the Irish have troubles!"

The class laughed. Encouraged by their laughter and my opportune arrival as an audio-visual aid, he embarked on his lesson with gusto. He broke into a spiel about the Black and Tans and how they were highly trained troops especially recruited by the British Government in 1921 to help the Irish solve their problems. Before he had got half way through I could feel my hackles rise. I put my hand up and said, "Sir," a couple of times, but he totally ignored me. His praise of the Black and Tans became so lyrical that my indignation reached boiling point. I jumped to my feet in such fury that I knocked my chair over with a loud clatter on the wooden floor

"Sir, my mother says the Black and Tans were a shower of thieves and murderers let out of English jails and sent to terrorise the Irish!"

The class were absolutely dumbstruck by my outburst at first and then they all started to snigger and talk at once. The history teacher was pretty annoyed that I had interrupted his lesson. He pointed a ruler at me.

"You, Granny …"

"It's pronounced Groin/ya, Sir,"

"I have no time to practise obscure tribal names. Who asked you your opinion or your mother's for that matter? Get out of my classroom and don't come back until you've learned to stop behaving like a peasant. As I moved towards the door he addressed the rest of the pupils. "This class knows about peasants. Don't you?" he asked, playing to his audience. "Tell, granny what we all know about peasants."

A forest of hands rose from the desks.

"You tell her," he said pointing to a fat girl at the front.

"Peasants are always revolting, Sir," she said.

The room erupted.

That's why they called me "the peasant" ever afterwards. I tried making friends although I knew it was useless. I approached a circle of less hostile class members one lunch break and asked if I could join them to eat my sandwiches.

"My you're awfy forward," came the sharp reply as they turned their backs and started giggling. For many months my presence served to bring members of the class together as they closed ranks against an outsider so that even the hangers-on and undesirables became part of the tight hunting pack. And I was the quarry. They bayed and snapped at every opportunity, imitating my accent, choking with suppressed laughter when I was asked to read in English and hooting with derision when I had to attempt to speak French. Any girl who wanted to ingratiate herself with the others only had to say to me, "I like your hairdo," or deliberately mispronounce my name and she was well in with the merciless, sniggering, shrieking pack.

Eventually I decided to fight back.

My name is Grainne, common enough in Ireland, but completely unheard of, it seemed, in the rest of the world. The boys of the class derived great entertainment from clutching themselves between the legs and calling out "groin ya!" whenever I passed. I eventually decided I'd had enough. I warned them to stop it or else.

"Or else what?" they sniggered.

I thought about what Pat might do and then waited my chance. Next time the boys had swimming I asked to be excused to go to the toilet. While they were all safely in the water I cut the crotch out of every pair of pants I could lay my hands on. It may not have solved the problem, but it was a declaration of war and gave me back a little bit of my old self.

The one area where I might have made friends was sport. But that too was denied me. I was only at the school a couple of days when we had PE. I was handed a hockey stick and sent out onto the pitch. Nobody bothered to tell me the rules. I supposed it would be much the same as camogy, the female version of hurley which is played fast and furious without too much concern for personal safety or the ankles of opponents. I raced down the field with my stick at shoulder height, hitting balls into the air and taking the odd wack at players' ankles when it came to a close tackle. The gym teacher was beside herself with rage and almost swallowed her whistle she blew it so hard. She kept shouting at me for fouling and eventually sent me off amidst jeers from the rest of the players. Needless to say I never made it into the hockey team, or any other team for that matter although I was reasonably skilled at netball.

In my third month at this new school, we were queuing outside a history room waiting for the teacher. The loudmouth of the class was standing in front of me in the queue, pulling long strings of gum out off her mouth, wrapping them round her grubby index finger and then stuffing them back in again. Suddenly she turned round and shouted at me,
    "You're staunin' oan ma tae,"
    "I'm sorry, I don't know what you're saying," I said.
    "You're staunin' on my fuckin' tae!" she roared
I leapt back instinctively as her false front teeth, attached to a horrible pink plastic palate, shot out of her mouth, propelled by the explosion of the f-word. They landed in my blazer pocket.
    "Thas better," she lisped through the gap where her front teeth should've been, trying to maintain the upper hand despite the difficulty

9

controlling her tongue and the reddening glow in her face.

I reached theatrically into my breast pocket and slowly withdrew the disembodied teeth with bits of fluff stuck to them. Then I pulled my cuff down over my hand so that I created a fat snake with two prominent teeth; a slithering snake that made hideous hissing sounds. One or two girls giggled nervously.

So I withdrew the snake, pulling it close into my body and then made it pounce at the pupil in front of me. She shrieked. The snake pounced again. Someone else shrieked! Pounce, shriek! Pounce, shriek! Pounce, shriek! Again and gain and again. The shrieks grew louder and shriller. Loudmouth tried to snatch the teeth. "Thas not sunny,"she lisped. But she sounded so funny I just couldn't help laughing. Once started, I couldn't stop. My shoulders shook, my eyes wept, I almost wet myself. Finally I slid down the wall in a helpless heap of giggles.

My laughter was, and always has been, infectious and in ones and twos and then in fours and fives others got struck by the giggles. Soon the whole class was sliding down the wall and wiping their eyes. And this was how the mystified teacher found us. Things were never as bad for me after that. Some girls became quite civil and we talked in the classroom about the subject in hand. I was even befriended by the fat girl who undertook to teach me to speak properly as she went to elocution lessons to "iron out her Scottish accent." Little did I realise at the time that this very friendship probably meant the kiss of death to any others that might have been budding.

All these memories fought for my attention as I tossed in the sticky hospital bed with the stiff, rubber sheets. Oh! To wake up in Ireland, to be back amongst friends in my civilised convent school. The nuns' singing lessons which were always old fashioned Irish songs like The Dear Little Shamrock had been a big joke to us girls at the time but now the words of The Londonderry Air seemed especially poignant to me and would become even more so as my near drowning incident made my life at school in Scotland even more miserable than previously.

A ludicrous heading in a national tabloid read: **SPOTTED GIRL ON BOTTOM OF POOL.** When I went back to school the "revolting peasant" now became "spotted girl."

And so I learned to despise everything about me that made me different and vowed to change my entire identity at the first opportunity that presented itself.

I started to make small changes to try to fit in. I grew my hair a little: I practised Scottish school slang. I even got nylons eventually. But I lived with the fear that someone would notice these changes and heap more ridicule on me. This daily nightmare lasted for two and three quarter years.

And then, quite suddenly it seemed, I was fifteen and free to leave school. No threat, however terrifying, no bribe, however large, could have kept me in that place a minute longer. Coming home on my last day, I binned my schoolbag and blazer with unutterable relief.

My first wages went on a lavish hairdressing consultation. I didn't just want a haircut: I wanted a whole new image. We decided on a simple classic look; dead straight with a square fringe, in blonde. The little kiss-curls that tend to stray round my forehead, especially when my hair is damp, would have to be brought under control with big rollers at night and hairspray during the day. The roots would have to be touched up every month. I made advance appointments there and then. Over the next few weeks my wages went on make-up. Again I began with a lengthy consultation and followed the experts' advice to the letter. My mother was annoyed and ranted on about "all the muck on my face" but I just ignored her. What did she know about looks or fashion I asked her, brought up as she was in an Irish bog and dragging up six children? She complained that I spent all my money on myself and paid nothing towards the housekeeping but, as I pointed out to her, I wouldn't have been paying dig money if I was still at school, which she had been begging me to do, so why should I have to pay it because I was working? We had so many rows about this that life at home became almost as unbearable as it had been at school.

CHAPTER 2

"And culled at noon the golden daffodils"
That came with spring to set the world aglow."

Now I was feeling very sophisticated as I left the
travel agents with the ticket in my hand. My new pair
of high-heeled shoes had increased my status as much
as my height and so I walked differently, with a
sinuous movement of my hips, just as much by design
as by the restrictions put on me by four-inch stilettos.
Looking back, I suppose "swagger" would be the
word that best described my walk. As, purring with
self-satisfaction, I looked at myself reflected in shop
windows and mirrors and positively hugged myself. I
had grown about an inch in the last year and had
finally left any worries about puppy fat behind. My
features had matured and the hamster jowls had
dropped away and left fine cheekbones, today
highlighted with blusher. Having left school I felt my
mother had no longer any right to stop me wearing
make-up. I thought green eye shadow and black
mascara made my eyes look stunning - my "smiling
Irish eyes" Uncle John used to call them.

When I thought of him my ticket seemed more
precious than ever. The last time I had seen him, some
three years earlier, he was waving to me from the old
grey house as I looked back, choking with tears,
before finally passing under the arch of laburnums.
He had been my special friend always. I could not
remember a time when he had not been around, or a
time when I was not his favourite girl. I hated my
father for taking me away from him. My smartly-
dressed, straight-backed, brutal father was such a
contrast to saggy, baggy Uncle John with his funny
crooked mouth that made him look like an old toy that

had lost some stuffing. He sucked a strange little briar pipe with a curved stem which he hardly ever lit. It hung loosely out of the side of his mouth as if attached inside. When I asked why he didn't smoke it he said it was for making pipe dreams. He would tell me his pipe dreams sometimes and I would whisper him mine, usually involving Pat Molloy in the starring role.

Pat and I had had many exciting adventures since he had rescued me from Wylie's pond; stealing apples, tying doorknockers together, climbing out of our bedroom windows in the middle of the night to lie on the shed roof and look at the stars. And worse.
Once when we were very bored we crept into an open house where there was a wake. Our only knowledge of wakes at that time had been gleaned from the song, "Finnegan's Wake" which made it sound great fun because all the mourners fall out and they have a big punch-up and a splash of whisky from a thrown glass brings the dead man back to life causing a powerful commotion.
But there was no commotion at this wake: just an endless procession of pious old women muttering prayers and sipping scalding cups of weak tea in the kitchen. The dead woman was very old and most of the people at the wake were in their eighties. We went into the stuffy parlour to look at the corpse. She had been a real terror to us alive, always telling us off in the street for making too much noise or embarrassing us in public places. Once she sat beside me on a crowded, bus, full of home-going workers from the Derry factories, and said to me in a loud voice, "When you get home tell your mother you've got worms. I can tell by the look of you. Tell her to give you a dose of sulphur and treacle."
Now, at the wake, we saw a chance of getting our own back and having a laugh at the same time. Pat

14

started to giggle as he leant over the coffin, pretending to kiss the old wrinkled face. He pulled open one of her eyes and left her with a permanent wink. I had to stuff my fist in my mouth to stop myself laughing out loud. Not to be outdone, I then leant over the coffin and drew back her mouth in a horrible grin. God knows what Pat might have done next if we hadn't been disturbed by an old man coming in to pay his last respects. We were sidling out the door, choking with suppressed laughter when we heard him scream. We shot down the garden path and hid in the old air raid shelter for most of the evening. For weeks after the incident Pat and I would pull hideous faces like the old dead woman's and collapse in stitches.

I was laughing to myself remembering it. And that led me to wondering idly what Pat would think if he could see me now.

As I passed a mirrored pillar in the shopping centre I caught sight of my recently highlighted hair and swung it back over my shoulders with delight. I had started ironing it every morning to get rid of my natural wave and achieve that dead straight look of Maryanne Faithful, the latest fashion. I was humming to myself and wishing that the boys at school could see me now. I felt sure they would wish they had never called me "the Irish peasant" or teased me about being revolting. Not that I was interested in any of them. In fact I felt sure that every boy I met from now on would see that I was drop-dead gorgeous and would be desperate to date me. And I was looking to meet exciting strangers when I moved far away from home.

Before I left school I had asked my English teacher's advice on how best to obliterate my accent. He was an old Watsonian himself and was quite in agreement with me that the only way to get on is to speak the Queen's English. He suggested that I buy records of Claire Bloom and learn to speak like her. The following January sales found me, therefore, hunting out such records. For months after that there was a fight every night in the house over the Dansette because I wanted to play Claire Bloom and my wee sister wanted to play the Beatles. Eventually, I was forced to buy a second hand player of my own in order to shut her up.

My efforts soon began to bear fruit and I realised I was making headway when the other girls in the shop started calling me "Lady Muck" and making references to my being "hoity toity".

After a year I felt the transformation was complete and I could start thinking about moving somewhere else to live; somewhere were the shadow of my past would not fall; somewhere were the new me would start a new life. But first of all I was going to see Uncle John. I had just bought a ferry ticket to Ireland. I was going back to visit the place where I once belonged.

CHAPTER 3

"Oh tarrying years, fly fast and ever faster"

Uncle John lived in the border country of Ireland where I had been brought up. It was a strange and beautiful and sometimes terrifying place where the people, because they could claim to be British and Irish, were neither, but rare hybrids of both. His house was in a hamlet only a few miles from the outskirts of the sizeable city of Derry in Northern Ireland, but part of his garden, across the road, was in the tiny village of Muff in the Republic of Ireland, another country entirely.

The border was a constant source of disputes which started in 1921,the day the British Prime Minister, Lord George, a Welshman, on holiday in Scotland, drew a new line on the map of Ireland. The line passed through the nine counties of Ulster and cut off six of them, creating the new British country of Northern Ireland and gave back the other twenty-six counties of Ireland, including three of the province of Ulster, to the Irish people. This impromptu changing of the map of Ireland at Inverness Council Chambers was meant to resolve the issue of home rule for Ireland and bring peace but in, fact, it provoked 40 years of civil war.

On the border, was, therefore, not a good place to live, politically-speaking. We might as well have been a lost tribe in the Amazon as far as modern advances in communication and sanitation were concerned. In the 1960s we still drew our water from a well and carried it in white enamel pails to the house each morning. We lighted our homes with paraffin lamps. A solid fuel range burned day and night to heat and cheer us. On cold winter evenings we toasted our toes there and bathed in a tin bath in front of its glow. Our clothes were smoothed with flat irons heated against the grate and washed in rainwater gathered in a barrel in the yard. We used to wash our hands and faces in the backyard in water from this barrel every morning before going to school. In winter this often meant breaking the ice on its surface first. Most mornings the washing of clothes would be in progress before I left for school and they would be drying on lines criss-crossing the yard by the time I came home. Only five miles away, in houses in the city, machines washed and rinsed and spun, but we had neither running water nor electricity and my mother, like all the others in the village, spent hours daily, slaving just to keep her large family in clean clothes and bedding.

Nearly all the families in the village were large. That's what made it such a fantastic place to grow up in. There were six children in our house, of which I was the fifth. My oldest sister, Molly, was nine years my senior, a princess in swirling dirndl skirts and red lipstick by the time I was seven. My little sister, Kate, was five years my junior and I remember having to take her out in the pram and chasing after her with a cloth when she went through a phase of peeing in the funniest of places. Each child in the family had several friends in the village of their own age and I can never ever remember a time in Ireland when I was stuck for someone to hang about with after school or during the holidays. At least not till I went to grammar school. The brains of the family, and the village too it seems, at the age of eleven I won a scholarship to a posh convent school (the first girl in the village ever to do so) and the year before we all went to live in Scotland I had the happiest year of my life.

The convent school was a converted country mansion set in several acres of natural woodland that dipped

18

and meandered down to the banks of the River Foyle. During breaks in lessons we were free to wander through the grounds where the leaves made patterns of dappled sunlight on the soft earthy paths whose colour and shape changed with the seasons. When I arrived for my first day the leaves of the beeches were dark green and full of summer. By Halloween they were already curling into millions of papery chrysalises which would hang on the branches all winter long. By Easter the first tiny lime green leaves were appearing, fragile and translucent as butterfly wings and as the days grew longer the leaves broadened and deepened in colour till they were rich green and swaying in huge canopies overhead, picking up the soughing south-west wind in ancient forest songs and roaring wildly in summer storms. Running like a wild thing set free, I would race through the trees, along the paths, down to the river surging to the sea. But before another spring came round the sea was to carry me away from that lovely place and all that I knew and loved.

My father was given Hobson's Choice: take up a post in Scotland in three weeks time or be made redundant. The first rumblings of "The Troubles" had shaken Northern Ireland and he, a Catholic who worked for the British Government, was considered to be a risk in his job.
In that year at the convent school, homework had kept me in of an evening so I drifted apart from my friends. But it was my expensive uniform, paid for by a government grant, which really set me apart from the village children. It consisted of a navy-blue gym-frock -St Trinian's style and old-fashioned even in the 1960s - a white shirt, navy tie and royal blue wool blazer. This blazer, bought several sizes too big by my thrifty mother, was quite the most expensive item I had ever worn and the envy of my older sisters who

used to borrow it without my permission to wear over summer frocks The summer uniform was completed by a navy gabardine raincoat and white ankle socks, the winter one a beautiful hooded navy nap coat with tartan lining and long thick black stockings. Because of these stockings shouts of "liquorice legs" from village kids followed me as I rode by.

And then there was the beret, to be worn at all times with the uniform, even out of school. The nuns had spies who reported you if you did not comply with this rule. I liked my beret and thought I looked quite distinguished in it, but it was like a red rag to a bull when I wore it in the village. This piece of headgear with its badge emblazoned on the front, set me apart as a snob. But I liked being a snob. And so my mother's stories of hiding her shoes in the hedge and going barefoot as a child because her school chums had no shoes, was lost on me. I loved my uniform. I had earned it and wore it with pride.

But now, forgetting any problems that my scholarship might have caused me, I clutched my ticket and went home to pack. I borrowed two enormous suitcases from the neighbours because I was determined to take all my best clothes and shoes with me and especially my luxurious towelling dressing gown which I hoped to get a chance to show off. Instead of helping me my mother watched me pack with a sullen face and prophesied all sorts of doom and gloom. She also kept asking annoying practical questions too, like how was I going to carry these cases on and off the ferry and down the last mile of road when the bus finally set me down. I hadn't actually thought of that. Uncle John didn't have a car and it would cost a fortune for a taxi, even supposing I could get one. I had to think long and hard about that one, but the answer, when it did come seemed obvious.

Pat Molloy. He was bound to know somebody. He knew everybody. He might even be driving himself by now. With a jolt I realised that while I had been growing up in Scotland, all my old friends in Ireland had been growing up too. I sat on my bed beside my suitcase and tried to imagine Pat Molloy at seventeen. But all I could remember was our parting. He had cried when I had told him that my family were moving. It wasn't a sobbing, wet cry like a girl's, but I saw the tears shine in his eyes like raindrops and heard the breath catch in his throat before he bolted away like a colt across the fields without a word, leaving me alone and bewildered. All the better, I thought, he's all the more likely to find a car to pick me up. I sat down there and then to write a letter. I would have to post it first thing in the morning and even then there would be no time for a reply. But I knew he would come.

All the way to Ireland on train, bus and ferry I thought about Pat Molloy and tried to imagine what he looked like now. But the only images I could bring to mind were of a twelve-year-old boy in baggy home-made shorts with scabby knees, climbing like a monkey and helping me after him, often turning round to me a freckled impish face with a wide grin and the biggest bluest eyes you ever saw. He was the best climber in the village when we were kids but I couldn't see that being much of a claim to fame at seventeen. I reckoned he'd be floored when he saw how I had grown up.

CHAPTER 4

"I long to see the vale I loved so well"

"

When I got off the bus Pat was sitting on a grassy
bank by the roadside and I wouldn't have known him
if it hadn't been for the eyes. They scrutinised my
face with a look that gave nothing away. His freckles
still showed but had weathered into that golden
complexion of fair-skinned people who spend most of
their lives outdoors. His hair had darkened to the rich
colour of newly ploughed fields and his shoulders had
broadened most handsomely. A slow smile began at
the corners of his mouth and spread across his whole
face, wrinkling up the corners of his eyes in a way I
remembered. But there was something a little
disconcerting, even mocking, in that smile which I
had never seen before. He stood up then and I had to
look up to him, tall and slender as he was, like a
young tree full of latent strength and vigour.

    "It's yourself then, Grainne Kelly." He said,
taking my hand.

    "Of course it's me," I said testily, "Who else
were you expecting?" For the coarseness of his accent
jarred on my nerves.

    "I wasn't expecting you to look like this," he
said.

    "I bet you weren't," I replied, stroking my
long blonde hair and giving him my fabulous calendar
girl smile.

    "Indeed, no. I don't think I would've
recognised my own mother under all that paint and
powder."
I felt a total fool. Tears welled up in my eyes and, not
knowing how to hide them, I took refuge in anger.

"The last time I saw your mother a bit of make-up wouldn't have gone amiss, "I said and stormed away, leaving him to pick up my cases.

He put them in the car and then followed me, slowing to keep pace with me, saying he was sorry and entreating me to get into the car. But I didn't trust myself not to cry so I asked him to deliver the cases to Uncle John's house and said I wanted to walk and take a look at the village. He didn't press me on the matter, just did as I asked. I was so upset that I hardly noticed the village as I crept through it and soon I was at the bottom of the gravelled path that led up to Uncle John's house.

On either side of the entrance the laburnums were in full glory, their cascades of yellow flowers sweeping down over the old gate. As I rounded a bend in the path I saw Uncle John waiting for me and, forgetting my new image, I pulled off my stilettos and ran up the path to throw my arms around him. But just as my arms encircled him I saw his face. It was the same face that I had always known, but now I saw it clearly for the first time. The scarred, sagging left jowl where the jaw had been removed because of cancer, loomed obscenely near me and I wanted to look away. The crooked, dribbling mouth sought my cheek. I pulled back revolted, pecked him on the good side of his face and hoped that the make-up would hide my embarrassment. All during the ritual taking of tea I avoided his eyes and hoped that the nausea would subside. I don't know which made me feel most sick, the sight of his poor face or my reaction to it. I might look beautiful but at that moment in time I felt a really ugly person inside.

If he noticed, Uncle John said nothing. But then he wouldn't, years of suffering had made him gentler and more tolerant than ever. He asked me about everything I'd been doing and showed a deep and genuine interest in my tribulations at school in

23

Scotland. He wouldn't allow me to condemn my tormentors though, saying mysteriously that everybody had their part to play in life and that maybe they weren't happy with the way things turned out either.

After several cups of tea I needed the loo and remembered with some misgivings that it was in the garden. When I got there I was horrified, having forgotten the disgusting smell of the primitive hole in the ground. As I sat on the wooden seat over this hole the wind blew in through the thin, slatted walls and I could see the garden through the spaces and the bits of newspaper threaded on cord fluttered in the breeze. No way was I spending a night, never mind a fortnight in a place with a loo like that. When I got back inside I chatted for a bit and then told my uncle I was going to stay at the local post office, which was also a B&B. I knew it wouldn't have a flushing loo either, but at least it would have a chemical toilet and I reckoned I could just about stand that. I could tell he was hurt but he spared me any embarrassment by not complaining. I left saying I would book in first and arrange for my cases to be picked up later.

I bumped into Pat just as I came out of Uncle John's drive. He seemed pleased to see me despite my off-hand manner earlier and so I asked him to fetch my bags to the post office. He looked puzzled.

"I thought you were staying with your uncle," he said.

"Have you seen the state of his toilet?" I asked, screwing up my face in disgust.

A spot of anger glowed in his cheek.

"If it's good enough for a decent man like your Uncle John it's good enough for you," he said and turned on his heel and walked away.

"You're the great one for sermonising," I shouted after him. "Maybe it's the priesthood you should be chasing and not girls."

24

He stopped dead. Turned round with thunder in his eyes.

"Chasing! Chasing!" He almost choked. "Who's chasing who? You're the one that's all painted and powdered like … like …"
I could see him search for a word.

"Like a whore!"
The word echoed round the hedgerows as I ran blindly away from him, leaving my cases lying in the road, my throat constricted with soundless sobbing. He came to my room with my cases and apologised the next morning, blushing and stammering, saying he hadn't meant "the word". He couldn't even bring himself to say it again. He didn't need to. It was still stinging as sharply and cruelly as the day I had first heard it. It was branded on my very soul. His distress as he looked at me was obvious: I hadn't slept much and my eyelids were puffy and swollen from crying; my hair hung in rats' tails and my clothes were crumpled from lying all night in them. He seemed at a loss as if he couldn't make up his mind whether he should go or stay. Then he moved towards the door and, just as he was going through it, he stopped and turned.

"Would you like to go for a bicycle ride on Sunday? He asked.

"I think I've outgrown bike rides," I answered peevishly and then I could've kicked myself as I saw the back of his neck turn scarlet before he fled.
Only on the Sunday did I realise what I'd done. Just after Mass a convoy of chatting teenagers set off on their bicycles as teenagers had always done all the years I had lived in the village. I remembered my older sister and friends in cotton summer skirts and dainty little white blouses pedalling off on such afternoons accompanied by the young men in their Sunday best. Some of these present young men rode two abreast with one hand on the shoulder of a girl. I

25

looked for Pat amongst their numbers, hoping it might not be too late for me to change my mind, but I couldn't see him anywhere. I did see his mother, though, and asked where Pat might be found. Her answer was mortifying. Pat had hours to make up at work because he'd had to take time off to pick me up at the bus stop and he'd decided to do it that Sunday morning. It had never occurred to me that he might have to work while I played.

"I'm sorry. I didn't realise …." I stammered.

"Don't worry yourself," she said, "he was happy to oblige. Sure it never did anybody any harm to oblige a body."

Her kind words and homely demeanour made me shudder at the memory of my comment to Pat about her appearance.

The cyclists began to move off in happy groups along the quiet country road. I stood alone until they had almost disappeared and the girls' skirts merged with the pink Campion and Lady's Lace by the roadside before I crawled off to my room where I purposed to hide forever.

I hated myself more fully then than I had ever done in my life. I was a stupid, ignorant, tarted-up fool, despite all the money I'd spent on my image. Because of all the money I'd spent on my image. Back in my room my image in the mirror made me feel sick. The blonde hair seemed false and idiotic. I looked like a doll, a stupid plastic doll. I rummaged in my bag till I found a pair of nail scissors and began to hack at my hateful hair, chopping it wildly and throwing handfuls of it over the floor. I would've kept on going till I was bald if my arm hadn't begun to ache too much. I even changed the scissors to my left hand in order to get more off, but finding I couldn't, I threw them down and began instead to scrub at my false, made-up face with a handkerchief. I rubbed till the skin was raw and

26

I couldn't see for tears. Then I emptied the contents of my make-up bag on the lino floor and ground every bit of it to pulp under my heel in a frenzy of self-disgust. Next came my clothes; those ridiculously foolish garments so silly in a place like this. I ripped and tore and shredded them, sometimes using my teeth as well as my hands, and threw them wildly about the room.

Then I fell on the bed physically exhausted with my head reeling, my whole body burning with shame. But I knew the ugliness was inside me and I could think of no way to tear that out. I was so distraught that if I had thought it possible to come at the ugly part inside me, I would gladly have torn myself open and plucked it out. Finally, I drifted into a nightmare-ridden sleep where witches with my father's face tortured me with burning sticks and the pupils from my last class stood around laughing. I must've cried out because I heard a knock on the door which so terrified me that I pulled the bedclothes over my head and lay shaking for hours.

I probably slept towards morning, waking long after breakfast had been served which suited me fine since I had no intention of ever eating again. I stayed in my room for two days like this, only creeping out for the loo and a drink of water when everyone was in bed. The landlady knocked once or twice. I didn't let her in but through the closed door I told her to clear off and leave me alone. It's funny but after two days of not eating you don't feel hungry at all. I had no plan other than to stay in that room forever.

But the landlady must've contacted Uncle John because he came softly to my door and asked to be let in. Feeling more ridiculous than ever I fell into a panic. There was no way I could face him after my recent behaviour and no way that I could let him or the landlady see the state of me or the room. He did not press me but said he would sit outside till I was ready to talk and not to worry about him because there were plenty of books and cups of tea in the house. Then he was silent.

After an hour of trying to ignore his presence, I was anxious to know if he was still there and called his name timidly telling him to go, promising to speak to him the next morning if he would just go home. I had some mad idea about running away in the middle of the night. I suspect he realised that because he very gently insisted that he would stay till I felt able to see him and to take my time.

The next hour I spent feverishly picking up the tattered clothes and bits of hair from the floor and ramming them into my suitcases and trying to clear as much of the mess of make-up as I could. But it was difficult without water. Finally I dared to look in the mirror. My hair was freakish, sticking up in tufts and bald in places. An effort to comb it had little effect. Then I allowed Uncle John in.

He threw his arms around me and held me close, hushing my attempts at apology. After a while he said, "Come on, you're leaving here. I'll get you a headscarf from Mrs Feeney."

I insisted that I would leave the room only if the landlady and everybody else kept well out of sight. I was capable of jumping out of the window I was so distraught. Loving and thoughtful as ever, he saw to this quietly and it made me hate myself all the more for the way I'd treated him. He had borrowed or hired a car with a driver and he helped me into the back seat and sat beside me. I didn't care where I went and didn't even look out. I was surprised, therefore, when we stopped to find that he had brought me to my old convent school.

We were obviously expected for we were ushered in to meet the Reverend Mother immediately on arrival. Uncle John seemed to have a tremendous regard for her and I sensed a bond of some kind between them

although I could not put my finger on. He said simply,
"You know Grainne, Mother Benedict, I think she
would perhaps like to stay here for a little while."
He looked at me for consent and I nodded. It was the
least I could do. But why he had brought me there I
could only guess at. He left us then with a warm look
from me to the nun and a polite bow. "I've got to go
now," he said, "Con's waiting, but I'll be back
tomorrow. On a bike," he added with a smile.
"Limousines are only for very special days."

And though I didn't know it at the time that was to be
one of the most special days in my life. A nun entered
carrying a tray of tea things and scones. I realised I
was ravenous and would've wolfed the lot if Mother
Benedict hadn't placed a restraining hand on my wrist
and told me to take it gently. I could've gulped down
a gallon of tea but she allowed me only three cups
before sending the tray away. Then she suggested a
walk.
Almost as soon as I entered the leafy grounds the
healing began. The ring doves cooed to each other
across the treetops A flight of bright finches,
undisturbed by our soft footfalls, danced in the air.
Wings fanned delicately, they swooped and circled,
their sunlit feathers the green of young beech leaves
in the spring. I wandered through the familiar grounds
for half an hour before saying a word to Reverend
Mother, waiting till the remembered odour of warm
earth soothed my nerves and the dappled patterns of
sunlight stilled my racing thoughts before I began.
I found my old headmistress as gentle and unchanged
as the landscape. She allowed me to talk, rarely
interrupting or commenting, prompting me only when
I faltered. I told her what I'd done to Pat and Uncle
John holding back only that first horrible,
unforgivable moment when I pulled away from my
uncle's scarred face. But she sensed that I was

holding something back and said, "Get everything off your chest now. It's like bursting a blister. As soon as you let the burning liquid out the pain eases and the healing begins."

I took a deep breath and told her. "His face turned my stomach. I couldn't bear to kiss him."

I don't know what I expected her to say. That he'd get over it, that he'd be used to it by now - arguments that I had already tried to ease my conscience with. But, she said something completely baffling.

" Believe me, I know how you feel. I've been there," was what she said. I looked at her enquiringly but she would not reveal more. After a moment's silence she started to speak again and there was a tone of deep sadness in her voice. "Poor child," she said, "don't be so hard on yourself. We can only be ourselves; limited as we are by our human flaws and the circumstances we find ourselves in. You would never willingly hurt your uncle. Your own feelings took you by surprise. Sometimes we don't get a chance to understand things before we act. Here you will have the time to mull things over and I hope you will come to the conclusion that you're not such a bad girl after all."

Then, putting her hand on my shoulder she asked quietly, "How are things with your father?"

I blushed scarlet to the roots of my hair. It had never occurred to me that she might know. It had never occurred to me that anybody outside the village would know. The shame flooded me again as it had done that very first time that I realised the village knew. I was only about seven then, on the way to school when a sharp stone caught me just behind the knee. Wheeling round I faced a big boy of ten or so.

"By god your da was giving your ma a bad time last night, was he not? Was he drunk or what?" I just turned round and walked deliberately on.

"He said a dirty word," he called after me.
I just kept walking.

"He called her a…"

I spun round. I could not let him say that terrible word in the street, in broad daylight.

"Liar," I shouted. "Liar. Liar. Your bum's on fire!"

"I heard him. He called her a…"

I got him once on the cheek with my school bag before my head hit the road.

"He called her a whore, " he sneered, "and you're just a dirty wee whore too."

I was silent for some moments remembering this and Reverend Mother squeezed my shoulder, "I'm sorry, I didn't mean to distress you. I thought it might help to talk about things. I put my hand up to where hers rested on my shoulder and touched it.

"I'd like to tell you about something," I said, "because I couldn't possibly talk to anybody else about it and they say a trouble shared is a trouble halved."

I'll never know where I got the courage to tell her about that last night before we left Ireland. It had become a recurring nightmare. My mother lay silent and unmoving on the hearth where she had struck her head hard when she fell. I thought she was dead. My older sisters were clustered round her in the mess of ashes and water pouring out of the grate. The enamel pail rolled on its side across the floor, echoing emptily. My father, in a rage, had thrown its contents onto the fire. The cat, limping from the kick he had given it, was pacing at the back door. Molly, my oldest sister, wanted to go to the phone-box at the head of the road to phone for a doctor but Father barred her way, shouting and brandishing his baton.

"I'm only going to let the cat out," she said although she had decided to make a run for it. He lifted his revolver from the shelf where it always lay in full view of us children and aimed. I screamed. Molly stopped in her tracks.

"Daddy!" I screamed. "Daddy!" and ran to him. I had some half-formed idea of knocking the gun out of his hand. He hit me hard across the face with the revolver and I fell backwards. Molly caught me as I fell.

"Get her to bed you useless bitch," he shouted at her and she had no choice but to comply. We hurried into the back bedroom without a word, too scared even to whisper about the terrible thing that had happened. I tried to speak, but Molly put her finger to my lips and whispered, "Mammy'll be alright."

Next morning the smell of bacon frying crept into our bedroom. My mouth was full of saliva and my stomach yawned emptily before I was even awake. I crawled out from between my two sisters who shared my bed, pulled a coat over my nightclothes and crossed the yard to the toilet. Then, like every other morning that I could remember, I scooped water from the rain-barrel with a tin basin to splash my face. This morning, however, I waited till the water in the basin was still and looked into it to see how bad my injury was. My face felt very tender and swollen. I touched it gently with the cold water and it stung.

When I entered the house my father was enthroned at the head of the scrubbed, wooden table and my sisters were sitting meekly round the edges. Mother was cheerfully serving him a huge plate of ham and eggs and fried tomatoes. My sisters were eating fried bread. I got the last slice and ate it guiltily, not daring to speak.

"It's a lovely day for the journey, Ownie," said my mother.

"Red sky in the morning is the shepherd's warning," he said and I shuddered.

32

Then he rose from the table resplendent in his uniform, took his revolver from the mantle piece and went from the room without a word. My mother followed him to the doorstep. He kissed her roughly on the bruised cheek before roaring off into the bright morning on his Royal Enfield motorbike, throttle fully open, bashing the silent hedgerows and raping the country roads as he went. Mother came into the kitchen and smiled at us. We ran to her, cuddling the bits nearest.

"Mammy, you've got to get out of this," Molly said. "We could hide till the boat's gone and then come back here."

"Shhh ... remember the little ones," she replied. "Remember, too, that he's my husband for better or for worse and where he goes, I go." Reverend Mother held my hand tightly in hers. You need to get out of there," she said.

Over the next few days she worked hard at persuading me to take up my scholarship again. I was still only sixteen and there were many senior girls in the school older than that. She was sure she could persuade the relevant authorities to make the necessary grants available again. Oddly enough, it was the thought of boarding in the convent that appealed to me. Given the mess I was in physically and mentally, I would gladly have hidden there for as long as I could. And the happiest days of my life so far had been spent at the convent school. The more I thought about it, the better the idea seemed. I wrote and asked my mother and was a bit hurt by her ready agreement although it was really what I wanted. Reading between the lined, I realised she was really quite glad to get rid off me. And so it was settled. I would resume my studies at my old convent school that September.

CHAPTER 5

"I long to know that I am not forgotten"

The second-hand uniform that Reverend Mother scrounged for me fitted like a glove. So on the first day of term, my face cleaned of make-up, my cropped hair neatly brushed, I looked every inch the convent girl - anonymous almost. And I was glad. I had to begin a year behind my erstwhile companions as Northern Ireland had a different diet of exams to Scotland. And I was glad of that too. It seemed more like a fresh start in a way. I worked hard, partly to honour the trust put in me by everybody involved in giving me a second chance, partly because I was boarding and there was nothing else to do, but mainly because I realised how much I cared for Pat Molloy, a true friend, who had always been good to me and I was sure I had driven him to despise me. The harder I worked the less time I had to brood on that.

Weekends I would spend at Uncle John's. I wanted to kiss the sagging cheek daily: I wanted to make myself confront the horror of his loo daily: I wanted to drag impossibly heavy buckets of water from the well across the road daily: do whatever was necessary to atone for my selfish, conceited, disgusting behaviour in the past. I would run fool's errands, scrub floors, cook, sew -anything - if I thought it would get rid of the ugly me inside. And I would find Pat Molloy and apologise for everything I'd said and done to hurt him.

I even made a brave sortie into Borderland Ballroom in the hope of finding him there, deliberated for ages over what to wear. I didn't want to look too dolled-up or trendy but I wanted to look attractive. I had no idea what the local girls would be wearing, except that it would be years behind the fashion. In the end I fell for "the little black dress" myth, believing that I couldn't go wrong with that.

But I looked like a crow amongst birds of paradise. The other girls wore brightly coloured summer frocks, nipped in at the waist and falling in soft folds to a wide hemline so that when they birled in a dance the skirts floated out around them like gay parasols showing off their slender legs. I had to admit how pretty they looked and how appealing they were in their artlessness. Even the lipstick they wore seemed only to enhance their fresh natural looks like corn poppies in a summer field. I gazed at them longingly knowing what I had lost. I was glad Pat was not there and did not see me looking so out of place amongst that happy throng of unaffected country girls.

After that I gave up looking for Pat, painfully aware that I didn't fit in: that innocence and artlessness cannot be learned like precociousness and charm. I buried my head in my books and found study surprisingly absorbing. Other worries too began to claim my time. My latest bout of self-loathing had made me sensitive to my mother's letters and to the realisation that I had been less than kind or even dutiful as a daughter. I began to write her long letters telling her everything I could about village gossip and making an effort to write amusing things to cheer up her day and make up a little for my years of self-absorption.

I wrote regular news items about a couple in the village who had a mixed marriage. The husband was Protestant and the wife Catholic. They were a silly pair and nobody took much notice of them except when their antics got out of hand. They had decided they would baptise the first child in the Catholic church, the second in the Protestant church, the third in the Catholic, the fourth in the Protestant and so on. The arrangement had broken down pretty quickly and only the first child, Tony, ever got christened at all. Every time they had a row, which was often, that poor child became the focus of their arguments which usually ended with the wife leaving (for only a short spell). My mother loved to hear all the latest details of these family feuds which were hilarious, especially on the occasions when the husband would pursue the wife shouting things like, "Take your little Fenian bastard with you." Only to lead them home hours later with words like, "Poor wee souls sure it's not your fault you were born to the whore of Rome."

I wrote, too, about my studies which were going well, but I was careful not to appear to brag and not to raise her expectations although I secretly hoped that she might one day be proud of my achievements if not of my character.

A greater concern for me was the realisation that Uncle John seemed to be getting tired more and more easily. Looking back I marvel at the super-human efforts he must've been making on my behalf on my weekends with him. By the end of term he was so ill that I begged him to go to the doctor and waited anxiously to find out what was wrong. The diagnosis was devastating. The cancer was back. I cancelled my intended return home for the summer holidays and moved in to look after him. That summer as the laburnums wept their silent yellow petals on the shingle path and the soft morning mists caressed the world, I learned what it was to truly love another. A chance to redeem myself had presented itself and I was determined to make the most of it. I got up cheerfully in the mornings to take him breakfast in bed. I used the best china I could find in the house. Sometimes I'd pluck a rose from the rambler by the door and put it on his tray. "Valentine's day again," he would joke. So that he could wash in comfort I would heat a kettle to fill the lovely old ewer belonging to my grandmother and carry it to his room standing in its matching basin with a pretty little Christmas-gift soap and one of the good towels which he kept for guests. Then I would leave him to dress at leisure. When he came down stairs he would listen to discussions or plays on the wireless until lunchtime unless it was a particularly fine morning. If the day was warm and still we strolled out together arm in arm at a very gentle pace. I always took his arm like a lover's because I didn't want him to feel like an invalid.

I learned more in that summer from Uncle John than in all the years at school. I learned not just facts, although he imparted a great deal of local and national history to me, but how to think and evaluate for myself. What I enjoyed most was learning about the world on my doorstep, the flowers, the animals and especially the birds.

"Take a look at that," he would say, pointing to a pair of robins, "he's built her several nests and now she's choosing which one she'll have. There's something to be learned there. I expect the female's got a bit more sense when it comes to choosing a suitable place to bring up young. He probably gets carried away with the view."

I learned to identify the different birdcalls; the raucous cry of magpies, the continual scolding of blackbirds and the wonderful full-throated songs of the thrush. I have always, since those days grown some berried shrubs for the birds and kept a patch of nettles for butterflies however small or formal my garden. Whatever help I gave to Uncle John in those days of his illness, I was rewarded for a hundred-fold by his company. I was happy to cook and clean for him. But I wanted to do so much more: to scrub floors on my knees, tramp blankets in the bath, dig the garden till my back broke; to sweat and ache and roughen my skin in order to get rid of that ugly person inside me. But Uncle John wanted my company, he said, and preferred me to read to him rather than do chores. I did what made him happy and it made me happy too.

One of the stories he got me to read to him was "The Seed And The Sower" by Laurens Van Der Post. It begins with the words, "I had a brother once and I betrayed him." The speaker's younger brother has a humped backed, a source of deep embarrassment to his older brother. Because he himself is so perfectly formed, athletic and handsome most people are attracted to him and set up expectations of him. They expect that everything associated with him should be beautiful and perfect like he is and so his life is dictated by what others want and this leads to the betrayal of his deformed brother for which he never forgives himself. And so the hump-backed brother finds contentment while the perfect brother is haunted all his life by the feeling that he is an "ugly person inside." Because his whole purpose in life becomes an unconscious effort to redeem himself, the strong, healthy brother throws away his beautiful, talented life in false heroics. The message of this story, so cleverly chosen by Uncle John, was not lost on me. My heart became light as thistledown and like the hunch-backed brother, I sang at my work.

Only when Uncle John dozed off in his chair in the afternoons did I feel sadness creep over me with the lengthening shadows. When I saw his poor deformed face and the lines that pain had etched on it I was overcome with pity.

He had been a vibrant young man, keen on dancing and fond of the girls; only twenty years old when the cancer had eaten away his face and youth and vitality. And yet, somehow, he had managed not only to adapt and survive, but to be contented and untainted by bitterness. In the early days after the operation he had

38

taken an interest in gardening which saw him through many, many lonely hours as he scoured books for information or leafed through pages of colour photographs planning what he'd plant when he had the strength. In the first autumn after his treatment finished he had planted the small bare twigs which were now the glowing yellow laburnums standing like cheerful sentinels at either side of his gate, welcoming all who entered there. He had also planted sweet-scented ramblers which filled the garden with perfume all summer long.

But he never danced or dallied with the girls again. His sweetheart could not bear to look at his face and had stopped visiting him before he left hospital. I was appalled by this and said I would stand by someone I loved no matter what they looked like, but Uncle John just smiled a knowing smile and said he hoped it would never be put to the test; that he had admired Deirdre for her honesty however brutal it seemed at the time. I imagined Pat Molloy with his golden complexion crumpled and grey like dirty tissue paper, his full generous mouth sagging in a permanent lop-sided leer and hoped, too, that it would never be put to the test. As Uncle John and I grew closer that summer he talked a lot about Deirdre and the dreams he had shared with her, and the dreams he hadn't shared with her, like waking up one morning to find himself whole again.

He did become whole again after the nightmare, but not in the way he'd expected. He tried to explain to me how contented he was, but he didn't need to. I could sense it everywhere; in the unpretentious comfort of his home, in his ability to live happily alone, in the pleasure he found in everyday things and especially in his love of others. So enveloped was I in that love that I began to feel worthy of it. For the first time in my life I began to genuinely like myself, keeping my hair shining and my clothes pretty just for me.

When the summer ended I returned to school. My results had been very good and Uncle John and my mother were both keen for me to continue my education. I did so on condition that I stayed with my uncle and travelled daily, not just because I knew he needed the care, but because I felt that I had a home with him. I would get up early and make breakfast for us both, every morning giving thanks that he was alive and I would have him for another day. This feeling of thanks-giving usually manifested itself in song and Uncle John called me his dawn chorus. It was such a change from my father who used to complain that I was, "too bloody cheerful" in the mornings and say ominously, "sing before your breakfast, cry before your supper."

In Uncle John's house I would usually continue singing while I raked the ashes in the big black range and tried to get a glimmer of red embers before adding kindling to get a blaze going. I would then put on fresh coal and know that he would have a source of warmth and cooking all day. Before school I would skip down the garden path like a child and cross the road to fill the bucket with drinking water at the well across the border and then come back to get my bike and books for school. I felt my life was like that in those days: before I left for school I was a housewife and carer, but as soon as my bike flew out under the laburnums I was a child again, whizzing through puddles with my hands off the handlebars, inhabiting another world.

Just at the beginning of October when the air was bracing in the mornings and the dew heavy on the ripe blackberries, I fell in with Pat on the road to school. He was cycling to technical college in the city and was late on the road that morning because his mother was unwell and he had to see to the younger children. Nevertheless he took a detour with me, seeing me right to the school gates. We chatted like friends who had not seen each other for a long time. It was how it should've been when we had met at the bus stop well over a year earlier. Pat seemed to be late on the road fairly often after that, beset by a whole plague of early morning misfortunes like Katie of Colraine. This just went to prove, as I said to him, that misfortunes never come singly. This also stopped me spinning downhill on my bike on the way to school with my hands in the air and my legs splayed out from the pedals in case he should see me and think me childish. But it didn't stop me doing it when I was sure he was nowhere around.

Just before the Christmas holidays when my hands were frozen to the handlebars and the road was rutted with ice so that I had to cycle very carefully, Pat came up behind me in a madcap way singing "Jingle Bells". Startled, my bike wobbled, hit a rut and tossed me into the road. The sharp ice tore my black stockings and the skin off my knees. The pain brought tears to my eyes, making me feel a fool again. He jumped off his bike and rushed to help me to my feet. As I felt his arms under my armpits I struggled to hold back the stupid, childish tears but a sob escaped. He gently turned me round to face him and his eyes were full of concern, more concern than the incident merited. I blushed and turned away. Still holding me under the left arm, he moved his other hand to my face, drew it close to his, and kissed me. I was so happy that I began to cry in earnest and buried my head in his chest so that he wouldn't see. This made him feel a fool and he began to mutter an apology.

"I'm sorry, Grainne ... I shouldn't have ... "

"Don't be," I muttered into his jacket. When he didn't reply I looked up and said, "I liked it …. the kiss … I mean the kiss…

"I didn't think you meant the toss in the road," he laughed

We both laughed then, and looking down and catching sight of my holey black stockings with the white, goosebumpy skin peeping through, we dissolved into helpless giggles and clung to each other for support just as we'd done so often as children, eventually sliding down to sit by the frosty roadside because we had laughed ourselves legless. Then he kissed me again, a long, lingering kiss that had waited who knows how many years to tell its story to me. Neither of us could think about study or books after that so we stole away over the border into that other country.

I will never know a Christmas like that again: the storybook wonder of it all. Pat brought us a tree which we decorated with lovely old glass balls and china angels that had been in the house since my grandmother's day. We decorated the main room with boughs of holly, thick with berries that year, I remember. As was the tradition, a large red candle was placed in the window and lighted every evening at dusk to offer hope and the promise of shelter to any passing traveller over the festive season. The house had a lovely warm cooking smell as I baked ham in cider, mince pies with cinnamon, Christmas pudding with brandy and mixed spices according to Uncle John's recipes.

At the beginning of the holidays Pat needed to bring the tree or an armful of holly as an excuse for visiting, but as he became more sure of his welcome he came oftener and just lifted the latch and walked in. My uncle was always as pleased to see him as I was and we would encourage him to draw a chair up to the fire and he and Uncle John would spend hours in deep conversation. Sometimes their voices were so low that I could hear the embers shifting in the grate and the ash dropping softly into the pan. I loved to see them in the warm yellow lamplight - the scarred old man and the vigorous young one so at ease with each other, the past and the present in harmony. They gave me hope despite the rumours of burnings and sectarian murders in the city.

There had been a terrible story in the paper about a baby in its pram outside a Derry supermarket being showered by the entrails of two young men whose bomb had blown them up as they were carrying it in. There was talk of civil rights marches and no-go areas and some people in the village who had grown up together were beginning to find it awkward to be in the same company. I knew all about the Black and Tans from Uncle John and I felt a silent terror that those days might ever come back. I looked at the two men I loved most in the world and wished that that lovely room was a sealed capsule in which we could travel to another world where there was neither sickness nor terror. One evening I saw Uncle John clasp Pat's hand in both his own in a very intense way and I strained my ears to catch his words. He was saying, "Don't be so headstrong, Pat. It's better to live for your country than to die for it."
My stomach churned as I was seized by a foreknowledge of doom. I knew there was going to be some black days, months, maybe even years ahead. These thoughts made me a little morose and when Pat kissed me on the doorstep as he left I clung to him longingly. I sensed how fragile was our happiness. I looked at the dark sky with its few brilliant stars and I knew that that Christmas time would be like that - a brilliant point of light to be remembered in the dark years ahead. A falling star etched a bright arc in the sky as I stood there, a symbol of hope, yet

emphasising our minuteness in the vastness of the universe, our mortality in the infinity of the world. I watched helplessly as Pat danced a daft jig of happiness down the glittering gravel beneath the star-dusted sky until he disappeared from sight under the bare laburnums. He was in love with life and with me and oblivious to the pain crowding in on us. I stood alone after he'd gone, heavy with knowledge like a tiny coracle, laden with hard-won silver fish, tossing in an Atlantic storm a thousand miles from land.

Eventually I felt chilled and went indoors. I was momentarily comforted by the cosy room till I saw the sweat on Uncle John's brow and the deathly pallor of his skin and I knew the bad times were already on us. I administered what comfort I could with a cool drink, aspirin and a cold cloth, but I realised the pain was agonising and he needed more pain relief than I could give. Reluctant to leave him, but desperate to get help, I shot off on my bike to the telephone box nearly a mile away. I was as sweaty and grey-faced as my uncle by the time I got through to the doctor. He was already in the house by the time I got back.

"It's time for the morphine, John," I heard him say as I came in. He had already opened his bag and was preparing a shot. I left the room and stood once more on the doorstep looking at the sky.

"Dear God," I prayed silently, "make me equal to this task."

The doctor came out and spoke to me in the same business-like tone he had used to Uncle John.

"This is just the beginning," he said. "It'll get much worse before the end. I'll arrange for a place in hospital."

"No," I said at once. And then I added hopelessly, "unless you can cure him."

The doctor shook his head. "You know better than that. Let me make arrangements. You've done your bit."

"Done my bit! What exactly do you mean by that?" I said through clenched teeth.

"You've been great. You've done all you could to make him comfortable … more than that … happy. In fact your efforts have been heroic."

"I have no desire to be a heroine. I simply want my uncle to be allowed to die with dignity," I said.

"In that case," he replied, "he would be best staying at home. But, I warn you, it's going to get rough. I'll give you all the help I can. But it won't be easy." He squeezed my shoulder and left.

I didn't go back to school after the Christmas holidays. I knew I might not be able to sit my exams or go to university, but I didn't care. It seemed of little importance when Uncle John was dying. Pat tried to persuade me to put him in hospital and then my mother wrote a furious letter addressed to Uncle John which I intercepted, thank goodness, because I recognised the handwriting and guessed at its contents. I did what I felt was right and risked falling out with them both. Pat came a lot, as usual, during January and talked to Uncle John in the old way. But, although I was always glad to see him, I didn't have time to linger with him on the doorstep when he left. When the first snowdrops appeared and I carried them to Uncle John's bedroom because he could no longer manage downstairs, I noticed that Pat's visits were getting shorter. He wasn't comfortable in the bedroom and was embarrassed by the sight of me feeding the old man from a cup, cradling his head against me and supporting his hand that held the cup with mine. Soon the visits began to grow less frequent and he might come once a week rather than two or three times.

By the time the primroses were peeping prettily out of the banks on either side of the path and the air was sweet with the scent of spring, we had stopped expecting him altogether. Or at least I had. I don't know about Uncle John. His periods of lucidity grew shorter daily and most of the time he was doped up with morphine to keep the terrible pain at bay.

On his last visit Pat had seen me holding a bed bottle while Uncle John used it. He couldn't hide his disgust.

"For God's sake put him in hospital, why don't you?" he said.

"I can't."

"Can't or won't?"

"I won't. He's dying, for heaven's sake."

"That's what hospitals are for."

"I want to give him all the comfort I can…"

"Comfort! He's getting that alright with a young girl holding his…" Here he made a gesture.

"You 're disgusting." I said. He's dying."

"He's taking a hell of a long time about it. That's all I have to say."

Pat glared at me with something like hatred and stormed out off the room.

At this time I did something I still wonder at. I don't know what prompted me to do it, but it seemed right. I wrote to Reverend Mother asking her to visit Uncle John. And for the last weeks of his illness she came nightly by car and sat an hour or two with him. She would nod to me on arrival and departure but otherwise she spent all the time in the house with him. Sometimes, if the pain had subsided enough, they would chat and I would hear the soft murmur of quiet conversation between people at ease with each other. I tried to arrange his morphine so that he could have the best period of the day with her. The night before he died she came wearing a pretty dress, stockings and kitten-heeled shoes. Although her hair was very short, it suited her that way and she looked lovely. My mouth must've dropped open when she came in because she smiled and put her finger to her lips. I distinctly heard him say, "Deirdre," before I shut the door and knew that my intuition had been right. I sent her word the next morning to tell her that he had died peacefully in the night and to thank her for her visits which had meant so much to him.

They had meant a lot to me too, compensating as they did for the absence of Pat in Uncle John's final days.

CHAPTER 6

"And there at home in peace to dwell"

Uncle John died on Easter Sunday morning. The first shafts of sunlight, so bright that even the heavy drapes couldn't keep them out of the room, squeezed in at the edge of the curtains and played upon his face, softening the pain lines and mellowing the scar. I wept for a long time although I was relieved for him that the pain was over. I knew the nurse was due at eight to give him an injection so I sat with him till then, holding his hand and talking to him in case his spirit still lingered in the room.

When we buried him the rain was falling softly and steadily, renewing the earth. They have a saying in Ireland that rain falling on the coffin is the sign of a happy death and I took comfort from that. The verges in the churchyard were starred with daises and daffodils bloomed on every grave. On the flowering currants diamonds of bright rain shone amongst the droplets of pink flowers and everywhere spring smiled and promised a new start. I was poignantly aware of rebirth all around me and Uncle John dead, never to come back again.

As a big arm fell gently around my shoulders and soft words of comfort sounded in my ears I turned to find Pat at my side. He led me back to Uncle John's house where his mother and other village women had prepared a funeral tea. I didn't understand how they could make tea and small talk when someone I loved was dead. They smiled as we came in and I realised he still had his arm around my shoulders. Numb with damp and pain I wanted to be alone. So ducking out from under his arm I excused myself to change my clothes. I went to Uncle John's room where the

women had tidied up and thrown open the window
and I slumped on the bed where he had died. After a
while Pat knocked and came in with a cup of tea.
Unwilling to be alone with him just then I suggested
we joined the others although all I wanted was to be
left alone. As soon as I entered the living room again
the questions started. Would I be going back to school
or would I be going home? How was my father?
They'd heard he was ill. What was wrong with him?
What was to become of Uncle John's house and so
on. I was not very forth-coming and was glad when
they all went home. Pat wanted to stay and keep me
company, but I was firm in my request to be left
alone.

But suddenly alone in that house after three months of
constant vigil and caring I had no idea what to do with
myself. I started cleaning fanatically. As I dusted the
mantelpiece I came upon his little briar pipe and
picked it up and turned it over and over in my palm
thinking of all the pipe dreams stored there in the tiny
bowl. I thought of Uncle John's favourite pipe dream
and as I did so smoke rings began to rise from the
pipe, drifting upwards and spreading till they filled
the room. They coloured like rainbows rings I had
seen shimmering over the blow holes at Fanad Head
and then gradually shapes began to form and turn into
figures. A crowded scene emerged. It was Derry and
there were dozens of Loyalist flute bands marching
round the walls playing The Sash. Down below in the
Bogside area Nationalist bands were marching too,
moving round the outside of the walls in the opposite
direction and playing Faith of Our Fathers. Suddenly
Uncle John appeared all dressed in white by the war
memorial in the Diamond. He spoke in a loud clear
voice, stilling all the players. He spoke of the world
wars and reminded them that Catholics and
Protestants had fought side by side in defence of their

country against a common foe. He asked them to
honour their dead who had fought for peace. When he
stopped speaking the bands on the walls looked down
to the bands below who turned their faces up towards
them. They exchanged military salutes and broke into
the tune of It's A Long Way To Tipperary. The
Nationalist bands moved towards the steps at
Butcher's gate and began ascending the wall while the
Loyalist bands moved towards Bishop's gate and
started descending. When the bands met they mingled
and marched on as one so that eventually there was
one huge band, about ten thousand strong, ascending
and descending from the streets to the walls and back
again playing a selection of universal evergreen tunes
and creating a spectacular sight for all the city to see.
I turned to witness what Uncle John made of all this,
but he had gone and a fountain played softly on the
spot where he had stood. The sound of water grew
louder and filled the room, The dream faded and I
heard the rain splashing in puddles round the house
and saw the windows running with water. I slipped
the little pipe into my pocket. I carry it always.
I knew then what I had to do. Forgiveness and
tolerance had to start somewhere. I decided to go
home and make peace with my father who was very
ill. There was still a week of the Easter break left and
I could come back to school afterwards. I knew that's
what Uncle John would've liked. But before I went I
wanted to pack away all his stuff because his was a
rented house. It had been lived in by members of our
family for a generations, but none-the-less it belonged
to some remote landlord. The clothes were easy. My
mother was always looking for clothes for a priest in
Barra, probably the poorest parish in the British Isles.
It was the small personal items that I had difficulty
with. Opening drawers and going through personal
things seemed intrusive and a breach of privacy. I
could now see the sense in cultures like Tahaiti where

a dead person's hut is burned with all their possessions inside. But Uncle John had all his personal documents collected together in a big envelope and clearly marked. His drawers had obviously been tidied out at some recent point. I realised he had done what he could to make this bit easier for me, sifting and discarding the clutter of a lifetime before he got too ill.

I packed the hideous Wally dugs -white china with gold collars and inscrutable grins - wrapping them in newspaper and burying them at the bottom of a tea - chest. Their smug smirks from the mantelpiece had irritated me continually during Uncle John's illness. Other ornaments I gave away to his friends as keepsakes. I emptied the oil from the lamps and started wrapping them up for packing too, but they were too beautiful to be consigned to the bottom of a chest and, on impulse, I put them in my suitcase for mother. His furniture I was at a loss to deal with, especially the old red velvet chaise longue which used to sit along the back wall of the living-room but which was now in Uncle John's bedroom. I think I was the only one who ever used that particular piece of furniture. But then I had used it enough for a whole family. When I was about four or five and forbidden to suck my thumb, I used to lie on it with a towel over my face and suck contentedly. Other times I used it as the boundary of my playhouse, a sleeping place for my dolls or a shop counter, for which purpose I covered it with old newspapers and odds and ends. It was old and saggy but I couldn't bear to think of it mouldering on a rubbish heap. Just before Pat's outburst about the bed-bottle, I had persuaded him to help me carry it to Uncle John's room so that I could sleep on it for the rest of my uncle's illness.

Suddenly I was overcome with terror as the room appeared like a torture chamber to me. My uncle's bed was the rack on which his poor body had been stretched for months - every creak in the night was the sound of the cogs turning, pulling his skeletal frame apart. The room was obscene with stifled screams and unshed blood. I saw that the ugliness of death had conquered despite all my efforts and fled from the house sobbing and ending up by the hearth of the nearest neighbour. He was a kind man and offered to see to the clearing of the house and the handing back of the key to the landlord. He promised to take especial care of the old red velvet sofa and make sure it got a good home.

I sailed from Derry to Glasgow that night. It was a nine hour journey which I spent sitting upright on a slatted wooden bench, travelling third class. The stench of cattle leeched up from the hold and their low, plaintive lowing became a constant and appropriate accompaniment to my sad thoughts throughout the night as the ship lurched and floundered in a heavy swell in the Irish Sea. Their wretchedness matched mine and my heart went out to them. Somewhere along the Clyde the poor brutes were unloaded at a special animal dock and then the ship took the human passengers into the Broomielaw where exhausted droves of wan-faced passengers were herded off. Many, like me, had long journeys still to face.

Much later, even more bedraggled after hanging about draughty bus-stations and enduring a two-hour bus journey from Glasgow city centre to Dunfermline and then catching a bus from there to Rosyth, I arrived home.

The expression on my mother's face told me how awful I looked. I hadn't considered till then what the months of tireless caring had done to me. But she looked so shocked that I was forced to take stock of my appearance. Months previously I had started wearing belts because my skirts had become so loose

that they were twisting round at the waist and I
couldn't find the pockets because they were
sometimes lying front and back instead of at each
side. I had shrunk my cotton bras by drying them over
the hot range. I had bought heel-grips for my shoes.
At the time, I thought my clothes had become old and
stretched from constant wear and not that I had
become thin. The mirror had told me I was pale, but I
didn't find that surprising since I had hardly been out
of the house for months.

Mother's initial look of pity soon gave way to one of
anger as she stood there in disbelief.

"In the name of God," she exploded at last,"
what's happened to you?"

I could think of no suitable reply and, desperate for a
cup of tea after a hellish journey, I blundered past her,
blind with exhaustion, into the kitchen and put on the
kettle. I had forgotten what squalor a big family
creates. I came back into the livingroom and,
removing an assortment of magazines, newspapers,
discarded clothing and hair accessories from an
armchair, I plumped down without even taking my
coat off. Mother went through and clattered about in
the kitchen, but after ten minutes when she didn't
come back into the livingroom I went through.

"Do you mind if I make a cup of tea?" I asked,
feeling like a complete stranger in my own home.

"Help yourself," she said coldly. "I hope you
don't expect me to start dancing attendance on you
now that you've run yourself into the ground looking
after that selfish old man."

I was too tired to argue. And I knew this mood of old.
From the earliest days I had realised that mother was
jealous of our love for her and felt threatened by
affection bestowed on friends, relatives or neighbours.
It was as if she felt that love given to others was taken
away from the capital sum of love that she had

invested in us. Boyfriends were the biggest threat of all and were very harshly treated None of my older sisters had ever had a boyfriend that came anywhere near the standards my mother set, not surprising since these standards seemed to be subject to change without notice. I remember Molly, trying so hard to please mother in this respect. She had been seeing a young man from an impeccable religious and social background - a "good catch" - to put it crudely, but mother thought he wasn't good-looking enough for my sister and went on about this constantly after he'd been visiting.

"   I can't imagine what a good-looking girl like you sees in a plain fella like that," she'd say. Or, "Do you think, will that redness round his nose get worse as he gets older?"

I once asked her what she'd do with a houseful of old maids since she was obviously dead set against any of her daughters marrying and she flew off the handle and said she didn't know what I meant, but she did lay off Molly's boyfriend after that, so I think she knew quite well what I meant. And she had often reason to wish that she had been less critical of the young men my other sisters brought home because the twins, Maryanne and Bridget, both moved away to work and married in secret when I was in my first term in Ireland. When my father learned this he banned them from coming home even to visit. I sometimes wondered guiltily if my stay away from home had encouraged them to try doing the same. I was aware that Mother missed them very much.

But in the weeks following my return after Uncle John's death her attitude to me did not soften. To be fair she was pretty exhausted herself because my father was off work ill and was very demanding. Apparently he had had a heart attack, but he looked perfectly fine to me. In fact he looked the picture of health as usual, lean and tanned his pale blue eyes -

the palest blue I have ever seen - hard and cold as ever. And, although he seemed to have stopped drinking, he was still smoking his forty Capstan cigarettes a day so I found it hard to believe he was seriously worried about his health. I thought he had probably just pulled another of his stunts and I said so to mother. She was furious and would've slapped me if I hadn't moved in time.

"I don't know what you're talking about," she said. But I think she did.

When I was quite small, about seven maybe, and did not fully understand my father's drinking habits or why sometimes, for no apparent reason, he would come home raging and start throwing the furniture into the back yard, smashing crockery and trampling what food was in the house into the floor, something happened that I have never understood or been able to forget. He had been raging as usual; this time about my mother's cooking and shortcomings in the house. He had grabbed a wedge of her home-made soda bread and stuffed it down his trousers with the words,

"This is good for nothing but stuffing up a hole."

This was one of my father's most frightening insults. Although we did not know exactly what the words meant, we did know that it was always a signal that violent acts were to follow. He had then thrown the plate through the window sending shards of broken glass crashing into the backyard and we children had melted into the darkest corners of the room. But instead of searching one of us out and beating us to a pulp as was usual, he had blundered off towards his bedroom. I don't really know what happened next or how much later it was because we children were used to cowering in corners for hours at a time. But I do remember a terrible commotion in the house and daddy lying flat on his back on the bed. Mammy was

55

almost hysterical, moaning and praying and sprinkling holy water round the room. She had sent Molly running for the next door neighbour and was shouting, "Grainne, Grainne, come here, for God's sake child!" Timidly I had crept into the room.

"Whisper an act of contrition in his ear," she had said. "There might still be time."
I had just knelt down beside the bed and begun whispering, "Oh My God, I am heartly sorry for having offended thee …" when Mrs Devine had rushed in, drying her hands on her apron. She had held a mirror to daddy's lips and said he was dead for sure. There was not the slightest sign of misting on the glass. They had lit blessed candles and put them at the head and foot of the bed and mammy had sent Molly for the priest and Brigid to phone the doctor. The whole family and the neighbours had got down on their knees round the bed and were saying the rosary and crying. But I was dry-eyed and very relieved like Jack when the giant falls dead out of the beanstalk.

They had been round the rosary several times before the priest arrived because it was a good long way to the nearest phone box and the Parochial House was even further afield. Father Lynch had already put on his stole and started preparing the holy oils for Extreme Unction when Doctor Kavanagh came. The doctor had taken one look at daddy lying rigid and waxen on the bed and motioned the priest to go ahead with his duties. Father Lynch had approached the bed and made the sign of the cross with holy oil on daddy's brow.

Suddenly daddy had sat bolt upright and said, "What the fuck are you doing? Do you think I'm dead?" Mrs Devine had fainted clean away and the other people in the room had frozen in terror. I have never been so frightened in my life before or since. My knees wobbled, my breath stopped and I peed myself.

The doctor had shooed us all gently from the room. "I must examine my patient in private," he had said matter-of-factly as if people came back from the dead all the time.

Mother would never discuss this incident and when I tried to describe it she would say, "I'm sure you must have dreamt that." But I know I didn't. Nor did I dream the endless nights of terror when I lay trembling, scared to sleep in case my father turned into Jack's giant and came hunting me in the night for being glad that he was dead.

Now I looked at my lean handsome father who was supposed to be seriously ill and wondered if he'd been playing more tricks. I could not understand at the time, therefore, the accusation in my mother's eyes when I set off at the end of the Easter break to finish the school year in Ireland.

The journey back was uneventful. Reverend Mother had arranged for me to be picked up off the boat at Derry Quay. It was the same car and driver used by Uncle John when he'd come to take me away from Mrs Feeney's and entrust me to Reverend Mother's care. Overcome with the memory of his kindness and the bitterness of my loss I wept silently all the way to the convent where I was to board till the end of the school year. There was a whole term's work to catch up on and the exams were not far away so I spent the next three months studying and sitting exams. Everything else was blotted out. When the exams finished, therefore, I was stunned. An abyss opened up in front of me. I had to face the question of what I was going to do with my life.

At one time I had it all mapped out. Now my earlier plans all seemed childish and pointless. What was the point of obliterating my past and going to live where nobody knew me? University, if I got in, might offer a respite. Then what? Yet what was the point of going home? I couldn't see me settling in at home again after the past two years in Ireland. I had changed but my family would always consider me vain and selfish no matter what I did. Even an act of heroism from me would no doubt be construed as an effort to get into the limelight. But I could not stay in Ireland. I had no job and no money. Worst of all I had no home and no chance of getting one. Flats or houses to rent were as scarce as hen's teeth in Northern Ireland in those days.

And so I left the convent for the last time that June full of silent despair, feeling that the most important part of my life had ended and the rest must be got through. The soughing wind in the leafy canopy overhead seemed to be intoning a lament for the end of my school days. The birds were chirping plaintively for their straying young who had flown the nest and were facing the wide wilderness half-fledged. Even the shining river seemed only a mirror for my sadness as I stood on the bank throwing in ivy leaves. I had pulled an ivy leaf, put it in my pocket and chanted the little rhyme which we used to say as children: "Ivy, ivy, in my pocket, who's the man I'm going to marry?" when I was struck with nostalgia for the early days of my courtship with Pat. I threw the leaf away and then threw others after it and watched the current swirl and engulf them, carrying them inexorably to the sea. I felt I had as little power over my life as those leaves and that it was just as worthless anyway.

I cycled forlornly along the summer-ripe roads, oblivious to the hedgerows full of corn marigolds, raspberry flowers and little creeping cranesbills, wishing only to take a last look at Uncle John's house. The laburnums poured their yellow cascade of flowers over the gateway just as they had done when I had

arrived on that fateful holiday visit two years earlier. I
stood there on the path encapsulated in that moment
in time as the yellow petals snowed softly round me
in a stir of warm summer air. I thought of how much
had happened in two years and the two men I had
loved and lost.

At last, picking up enough courage to move towards
the house, I threw my bike down on the gravel and
walked, head bent, treasuring the sound of the shingle
underfoot. I wanted to drink in every sensation of that
house and garden so that I could store them away in
my memory bank and take them out and turn them
over in my mind's eye like secret treasure during the
many years of emotional bankruptcy which I was sure
lay ahead of me.

Slowly I became aware that there was something
different about the path - sunlight in parts where there
had always been shadow. I looked up to gauge the
angle of the sun. And found that the house had gone.
The beautiful garden lay under a pile of rubble. The
lilac, heavy with bloom had been uprooted and lay
dying. The lilies had been flattened by huge wheels.
But the ramblers had twined themselves amongst the
broken masonry and were blooming profusely,
softening the ugliness of destruction and scenting the
air with their sweet fragrance as if in memory of the
one who had planted them. And sitting amongst the
roses was Pat Malloy.

Involuntarily my heart stirred, but my head told me
this love affair was as ruined as the house. I sat down
beside him and the conversation was as awkward as
the first time we'd met at the head of the road when
he had come to carry my bags. He smiled wanly at me
and told me that he came there often "to think about
things." I didn't ask him what these things were
because I guessed what they might be and I didn't

want to know. He seemed to realise this because he changed his tone completely and said,

"It's terrible this…. The house, I mean." I nodded. "Bloody landlords think they can do what they like."

"I suppose they can do what they like with their own property." I said.

"They think they can do what they like with the whole bloody country.
I did not reply. The last thing I cared about at that time was politics. But Pat persisted.

"You know what he'll do now, the landlord, don't you?"

"No," I said.

"He'll build about half a dozen houses and…..

"Sounds OK to me, there's a shortage of houses in this area."

"Sounds OK to you!" he shouted. Don't you care what happens to your country?"

"Of course, I care. That's why I think it's a good idea to build more houses here even though it means the ruin of Uncle John's garden. And he wouldn't have minded either. I'm sure of that."

"But building houses like this doesn't help, don't you see?"

"No, frankly, I don't and I don't much care either," I said getting exasperated. I just wanted to be left alone with my thoughts.

"Don't care!" he roared so loudly that I almost jumped out of my skin. Don't care! No wonder the country's in the state it's in when intelligent, educated people like you don't care about injustice or basic human rights."

"Now, hang on a minute! Who said anything about injustice or the violation of human rights?" I asked testily.

"The whole issue of housing involves human rights: every human being has a right to shelter and...."

"I know that," I interrupted, "but if the housing is simply not there...."

"Let me explain what I mean," he said in a conciliatory tone. "I see you don't understand the situation here after all."

I resigned myself to listening and sat down beside him amongst the rubble.

"We live in Northern Ireland, which is part of Great Britain, agreed?"

"Yes."

"In the rest of Great Britain every man and woman over the age of twenty-one has the right to vote, agreed?" I nodded, reluctant to be drawn in.

"But in Northern Ireland in this year, 1966 AD, only a householder has a vote."

"So that means that your mum can't vote, only your dad?"

"That means that my ma can't vote, my sister Bernie, aged twenty-three, can't vote, my sister Cassie, aged twenty-one, can't vote and I won't be able to vote even when I've reached my twenty-first birthday!"

"But that's not right!" I said, genuinely shocked.

"And that's not the half of it," he said

"Because only a householder can vote. That's why there are no houses available to Catholics in this area. We live in an area where the Catholics outnumber the Protestants two to one, yet almost the entire city council and police force are Protestant. The only way to change that is to have a say in local government. To get that you need a vote. To get a vote you need a house. But there are no houses."

"But you just told me that the landlord is putting half a dozen on this site - that's five more voters."

"A drop in the ocean! The fat-cat Protestant landlords make a fortune renting out houses like these. There'll be twenty couples after every house and they can charge as much rent as they like.

"But what's to be done?" I asked, drawn in in spite of myself.

"Protest," he said. "Non-payment of rent, marches, civil disobedience.

"Is it worth dying for?" I asked, remembering Uncle John's words.

"Who's talking about dying?" he said.

"I know my history: I've learned that the rich and powerful will kill rather than give up what they have. "

"I would die if I had to," he said, "for the good of the people of Ireland."
His eyes burned with " the terrible beauty" of youth which has found its cause. I felt then he was doomed to some high glory and an early grave. So disturbed was I by this that I stood up to leave, knowing he'd found his means of redemption as I had found mine. Realising my intention of going, he hurried after me and just as I got to my bike he caught me up in his arms.

"Did you ever think we'd get married?" he asked, his voice husky with swallowed tears.

"Of course, I did," I said warmly, "but…"

"Don't!" He put his finger on my lips. "Don't. I know. I threw it all away."
Then he drew me into his arms and kissed me with such love that he took my breath away. The world spun about me so that the sky, the earth and the falling petals were a spinning drum of colour with Pat and me at its centre. When we had to finally part our lips to take in air we held each other so tightly that

our bodies touched from head to foot and our arms were wrapped around each other like honeysuckle round a tree. We stood some minutes like that, recovering our equilibrium and I thought how ironic it was that our moment of deepest understanding should be the moment of parting. I was poignantly aware that the little yellow petals falling softly around us would be the only confetti we would ever have. I broke away lest I should succumb to some silly impulse to try again. I got on my bike resolutely and shot out under the laburnums. I had started to cry and didn't want him to see. I'm sure he stood watching till I was a speck in the distance. But I didn't look back.

CHAPTER 7

"Oh, Danny boy, the pipes, the pipes are calling."

Before I left Ireland for good, I had one more call to make. I had made friends with a girl called Mary Tolan in my last term at school. Like me she had come to board that term and like me she was a bit of an outsider. There was always a cool reserve on the part of most fee-paying pupils to scholarship girls because they were seen as socially inferior. Mary was not a scholarship girl, intellect was not one of her strengths, that wasn't the problem. But Mary's problem was, like scholarship girls,' one of class. There were a number of girls at the school who were intellectually challenged, and whose families had money and paid for them to attend. Mary was one of these. Her family were well-off, but her father was not a farmer or businessman. He was a bookie. Although they lived in a lavish house only a mile or two from the convent, Mary had come to board because her doting father thought it would somehow make her one of the girls. Most of the boarders came from far-flung farms in the south.

Mary was the timidest person I had ever met. She even looked like a mouse with her sleek, light brownish hair and small bright eyes which were so dark and restless that they gave the impression of a frightened animal about to bolt. Reverend Mother had no doubt put her in to share with me in the hope that I might befriend her. The first evening she stayed she sat on the edge of her bed after supper and twisted her handkerchief into a sweaty rag in the palm of her hand. I wasn't sure what to do. To put my arm around her and comfort her, which was what all my instincts told me to do, seemed a bit patronising. After all she had been a pupil at the school longer than I and was about my age. I thought of asking if she was missing home but I felt sure that would produce a flood of tears. In the end I resorted to fooling about.

"Mary," I said, "loosen up. This is just as much your room as mine. You can even fart in here if you want to."
She laughed and was a little more at ease. But she did not contribute any words to fill the empty silence left when the laughter faded. This silence forced me to talk.

"Tell you what, lets draw up a list of does and don'ts."
I said this to get her to move for a pencil and paper and hoped she'd stuff that sweaty hankie in her pocket. But she looked even more uncomfortable than earlier and screwed the hankie into an even tighter, sweatier twist.

"I'll start," I said with rising panic, realising I'd somehow upset her, and I took a bright yellow page-divider out of my folder and wrote in red pen; NO HANGING NAKED OUT OF THE WINDOW EXCEPT ON SUNDAYS.
Mary laughed out loud, thought for a moment and then got off the bed. She took the pen from me and wrote; BOYS MUST BE KEPT UNDER THE BED TILL AFTER LIGHTS-OUT. I followed this with; NO NAKED LIGHTS WHILE FARTING IS IN PROGRESS and Mary shrieked so loudly that a quiet voice at the door told us to settle down a bit. We carried on making our silly rules in conspiratorial whispers after that and by the time we fell asleep we had become firm friends. I spent many evenings teaching her how to pluck her eyebrows and French-pleat her fine straggly hair. It took ages for her to get the hang of it. But she showed even greater patience when she taught me to swim properly. Mary went home at weekends. She lived only a few miles away

65

in a big, showy house in town. I started meeting her in town on Saturdays to go swimming. I wanted so much to overcome my fear of water, a hangover from the near-drowning when I was thirteen.

I will never forget the first Saturday morning we went swimming. I was standing in the changing room in one of Mary's costumes. It hung about my puny thighs like a limp dishcloth. I had to knot the straps at the back because the neck plunged almost to my navel. My skinny white arms were covered in goosebumps. Only then did I realise just how thin I had become in the previous months. I was totally miserable and wondered why on earth I'd put myself in such a situation. The muted clamour of many voices coming through the showers sounded to me like an impatient crowd at a circus and I had no doubt that Mary and I were the clowns. But she seemed really excited and kept telling me to hurry up.
And there was only one clown in this circus As soon as we got to the poolside, Mary dived neatly into the water and swam gracefully around waiting for me, metamorphosed from mouse to mermaid. I crept tentatively down the steps at the shallow end and stood shivering, up to my waist in water. And she showed the patience of a saint in dealing with my fear. By the time I came to leave school and Ireland I was a very competent swimmer.
So now I was off to say good-bye to her with a sad heart with no idea when we might meet again. After the summer she was to start her nurses training at Altnegalvin Hospital in Derry and I was to study English at Edinburgh University.

When I rang the bell a very-good-looking guy answered. He was much darker in colouring than Mary but there was something about his eyes which instantly made me recognise him as her brother. He was very charming as he ushered me in.

"Sit yourself down," he said. "Would you like tea or coffee or something?"
I shook my head, lost for words for a change.

"Now what can I do for you?" he asked.
I was just about to say I had called to see Mary when she came bursting into the room.

"Was that the door … Mick why didn't you call me … ignore him Grainne…" Mick had turned scarlet and was obviously searching for some word or other when Mary burst out laughing.

"Oh God," she said. "You didn't think she was … Ah Mick. for God's sake wise-up … does she look like … Ah never mind … Come on, Grainne we'll sit through here."
She took my hand and towed me off to another room, cosier but no less magnificent than the one we had just left.

"What was all that about?" I asked.

"He thought you had come to talk about your problems …. He's in the Saint Vincent De Paul Society." I looked at her blankly. "They're a charity who do all sorts of things."

"Oh, I know who they are, but I thought they collected old furniture for the needy and gave hampers to widows and orphans and that kind of thing."

"They do that too. But a lot of their work involves counselling, you know people with problems, alcoholics…"

"I wonder what he thought my problem was?"
Mary laughed. "Let's ask him, shall we?" I jumped up protesting but she had already run out of the room laughing and she returned quickly, dragging Mick by the hand.

"So tell us, Mary teased, "what did you think her problem was?"

"Well," said Mick, trying to keep a straight face, "she has this terrible little fiend, I mean, friend, who doesn't show any respect to her older and wiser brother…"

"Ah, go on, tell us what you thought," Mary persisted.

"I thought what a good-looking girl. I wonder has she any older sisters "
It was my turn to blush and Mary, sensing my embarrassment, started pushing Mick out of the room saying,

"She has as a matter of fact, but they wouldn't be got dead with a goody-goody like you."
I thought of Molly.

"Doesn't he have a girl-friend?" I asked.

"Not yet. He's just home. He was studying for the priesthood, but they've told him he doesn't have a vocation. Ma's furious."

"Why?" I would hate my son to be a priest. Just imagine it: God, you'd have to be on your best behaviour all the time. No hanging out of the window naked, that's for sure!" We were rolling about laughing at this when Mick came back.

"Cup of tea, girls," he said, putting down a tray with tea things and cake and making for the door

"Why don't you join us?" I asked. Mary shot me a funny look, but I pretended not to notice. I was scheming madly. I just thought he would be the perfect match for Molly and I was getting worried about her: twenty-seven and not married.
Derry has a famous dog-track called, appropriately enough, The Brandywell, and many men in the city kept greyhounds. Betting on dogs was a favourite pastime, even amongst priests. I mentioned all the dogs I'd seen on the street and Mick became quite animated.

68

"There's a brilliant dog track in Edinburgh called Powderhall, have you ever been there?" I asked.

"No, but I wouldn't mind going. A lot of dad's mates have gone to the dogs there. Wouldn't mind doing it myself."

"Well, in Scotland at New Year most people go to the dogs in one way or another. At Powderhall there's a weird race at New Year, when men run around the dog track. It's a handicapped race and attracts fierce betting. The competitors train secretly for months beforehand wearing balaclavas."

"The famous Powderhall Sprint. I'd love to see that."

"Why don't you come over and see it this New Year? You could stay with us."

"It's a deal!" he said shaking my hand. When he left the room Mary looked at me in a puzzled way.

"Are you chatting up my big brother, by any chance?" she asked.

"God no, he's ancient," I said, "at least twenty-five. I think he'd suit my oldest sister." We started to laugh again and I hoped, hearing it, Mick would not think we were laughing at him.

I was a little tearful when I parted from Mary. It had been such a long time since I'd had a friend of my own age that it was a genuine wrench. She promised faithfully to come and see me in Scotland and to write every week. I still have all her letters.

And so my journey back to Scotland was again a forlorn experience, though this time at least, thanks to Mary's swimming lessons, I was looking and feeling much fitter. I arrived back to find my father had been rushed to hospital with another suspected heart-attack and mother was feeling as fraught as ever. Exhausted as I was, I accompanied her that very evening to visit him in hospital in Edinburgh.

It was an awkward journey although the distance as the crow flies is only about fifteen miles. We had to catch three buses which seemed to have been deliberately time-tabled not to connect which meant hanging around at bus stops for ages. .But at least it afforded me a chance to talk to my mum on neutral ground. We talked about my father. He was to have tests to decide whether or not they could unblock a furred-up artery in his neck. I tried to put myself in mum's shoes but I couldn't imagine loving a man who had spent his life abusing me and who had doled out good times in small measures like pokes of sweets that could be snatched back at any wilful moment he decided. I thought if I was her I'd be willing him to die. She sensed my difficulty and said, "I know life with your father isn't all roses and sunny lanes but…

"Who's asking for roses and sunny lanes? I would just like him to have loved us a little. He behaves as if he hates us most of the time."

"It's just his way. You mustn't take it to heart. A lot of men find their children a trial. There are good times too. Try to focus on those. Remember when you were in hospital getting your tonsils out and… "

"He came to see me every day. He wore his uniform and I was so proud. He brought me a proper box of chocolates, not sweeties like all the other kids' dads."

"Remember he bought us the first television in the village."

"How could I forget! It ruled our lives even more than he did! A word spoken during the news earned you a thick ear and a cough during Dixon of Dock Green meant a hiding afterwards."

"I'm sure you're exaggerating. It wasn't that bad. He just wanted peace to watch the television, that's all."

"There you go, making excuses for him as usual.

"He's never been a happy man. The war changed him. He feels guilty. He had a safe clerical job because of his ulcer."

"Mother you must be the biggest hearted woman in the world to excuse all he's done on those grounds. He's certainly made sure everybody else is unhappy."

"Grainne, he isn't always bad. He plays the flute beautifully. Remember how he used to play when you were little? Anybody who can make music like that has to have a soul."

"Don't talk to me about that flute! It gave me the creeps. I can remember coming up the garden path and hearing those beautiful eerie tunes he used to play. They were so sad they were frightening. I used to steal into the house and creep along close to the wall and sit in a corner to listen wide-eyed and enchanted … but scared … like a snake might feel when the charmer is playing…. Or the children who followed the pied piper."

"Too much imagination, that's your trouble."

"I suppose its my imagination that he burnt your…

"Forgive, Grainne. You've got to learn to forgive.

A silence fell on us after this and we sat side by side, each wrapped in our own thoughts till the bus got to the hospital.

When we arrived at his bedside I was surprised to see my father look as hale and hearty as ever. He was a little paler perhaps, but he did not look like a dying man to me. I had made up my mind on the last stage of the bus journey to forgive as mum said I should. After all people do change and my father deserved the same chance as anybody else. But my resolution faded as soon as he opened his mouth.

"You're late," were his first irascible words. "What kept you? Visiting time's half over."

It had, in fact, just started but that was typical of my father. I looked hard at him and tried to smile, but I was thinking, you bastard, you know what the journey is like and you know how tired we are. He was up tight because the tests had shown that all his arteries were hardening and there was no point in operating. He was to be allowed home the following day. The hospital had prescribed warfarin to thin his blood. There was nothing more they could do.

When my father had been back home for a few weeks things settled into a routine which revolved around him as usual. The weather was fine and he walked quite a bit, trying to make up for the years when he didn't bother about fitness. We all loved those hours when he was outdoors because we could relax, put our feet up even, instead of being tense, ready to spring into action at his beck and call. Molly helped mother as much as she could when she got home from work, making herself father's slave every evening after working in a factory all day. But Rosaleen, three years my senior and coming up to her twenty-first birthday, stopped in of an evening only long enough to eat and beautify herself before going out with friends. I was amazed that she got away with this because the older girls never had. Looking back, I realise now that this was a sign of my father's illness.

Rosaleen was a big, well-made girl with a very headstrong nature. He had in a way been more cruel to her than to any of us. I remember when she was about thirteen and had grown quite suddenly into a gangly teenager with a big nose and spots, he had turned to her one morning at breakfast as if he had only suddenly become aware of her.

"How did I ever father an ugly big bitch like you?" he had asked with genuine puzzlement. Now he seemed almost afraid of her. This became evident later that year when my mother was away for a few days.

The twins, who seemed to do everything in tandem, had even managed to be pregnant at the same time and were both about to give birth that autumn. My mother overcame all her reservations about leaving my father and braved his foul temper so that she could spend this time with her daughters and see her first grandchildren. Molly went with her and Kate insisted on being taken along. Father was to be left to the care of Rosaleen and I for nearly a week. I faced the task with trepidation, but Rosaleen faced it with glee. As soon as my mother was safely on the bus to Aberdeen she took over.

"Let's start preparing tea for the old bugger," she said.

Mother had left food and detailed instructions because my father was very choosy. There was to be a rare steak, wild mushrooms and four small, floury potatoes. Rosaleen took a tin of beans out of the cupboard and opened it.

"He doesn't like beans," I said.

"I know." was all she replied.

She emptied the beans into a saucepan and warmed them, then left them to stand while she toasted the heels of the loaf. She spread these thickly with margarine which he hated and then put dollops of cool, congealed beans on them and served them up.

"I hate beans," said father, "You know I do."

"That's all there is," she said, making to take it away.

"I'll try it," he said, holding on to the plate.

Next day he got the steak, but charred, and the mushrooms barely cooked. Before cooking them Rosaleen had juggled with them and dropped half a dozen on the floor where they picked up a few dog hairs, before she scooped them into the pan unwashed. He didn't say a word.

"I'll have the old bugger house-trained before mammy gets back," Rosaleen said, tossing pancakes to the flaking ceiling where they stuck and were peeled off with some of the paint attached and returned to the pan. I thought it was all very amusing but I was terrified of the backlash which I was sure would come.

I started university that week mother was away. It was Fresher's week and I was determined to make the most of it. On the Friday night I ventured to a disco and missed the last bus home. I managed to get the last train to Inverkeithing but had to walk the final leg of my journey to Rosyth. Father was waiting for me, his face full of thunder.

"I'll swing for you yet," he roared before I got through the door. "You young tramp, where've you been till this hour?"

He was about to grab me by the hair when Rosaleen appeared right behind him.

"Leave her," she said. He swung round and saw the stiletto-heeled shoe poised over his head.

"Get to bed," he growled and retreated.

I knew she was not being vindictive for her own sake, but trying to make him pay for years of cruelty to all of us, especially mother. There were times when he had thrown food at the walls, smashed plates on the floor and burnt mother's face with food that had been served up too hot. So I didn't interfere. I was very disturbed by her behaviour just the same.

But when mother came back it was worth it to see her face as my father threw his arms around her and said, "Bridie, darling, it's so good to have you home."

There was no mistaking the sound of genuine relief in his voice. Rosaleen winked at me and we enjoyed our secret triumph.

I started classes at university soon after that and I
moved into Edinburgh, glad of the excuse to get out
of the house. Under Rosaleen's guardianship things
were quieter between my parents and this took away
some of the guilt I felt about leaving. Nonetheless, my
mother was angry with me for going when the
university was within travelling distance. Yet it was
that very move that finally led us to an understanding
of each other. I persuaded her to come into Edinburgh
to do her Christmas shopping that year which we so
enjoyed that it was the beginning of many shopping
sprees together.

Molly had taken over mother's role with my father
more and more. I was grateful to her for allowing
mother to get more freedom, but I was very uneasy
about what was happening to Molly's life. When I
was seven she was a sixteen-year-old princess in
swirling skirts and red lipstick. She cycled cheerfully
off to work in the city every day, meeting up with
other village girls on the way, chatting and laughing
as they bowled along. She brought wages home which
mother was very grateful for. On Saturday nights
mother gave her some of the money back to go
dancing. She would come home flushed and happy
and tell us all about who was there and what they
were wearing and which fanciable young men had
danced with her. Her life seemed incredibly exciting
to me and I knew when I grew up I wanted to be
exactly like her. Now I was eighteen and Molly was
twenty-seven and her life was one of slavery. She
worked as a machinist in a factory where chatting was
not allowed and every penny had to be earned with
sweat She came home and would hardly get her coat
off before my father was looking for her to make him
a cup of tea because no one could make tea like Molly
he would say. Later he would get her to trail up and
down stairs for various things like his glasses or a

warmer sweater or some other pretext. He would
demand that she came and sat with him to watch
programmes which had no possible interest for her;
things like University Challenge and Pot Black. She
had given up going out in the evenings and did not
have friends home. By far the prettiest of all us girls,
she had lost her sparkle and was becoming a drudge. I
knew father was a tyrant but I could not understand
why he had so much power over her. Then one
evening I heard him shout at her to go and wash. He
said she had BO. She apologised and said she'd go
and wash but he said she needed to shave her
underarms to stop the problem of BO properly. She
said meekly she would do that too. Then he said that a
razor was no tool for a woman to use and he would do
it for her. Molly looked at mother who inclined her
head very slightly. She gave in with a sigh of
resignation. I knew I had to get Molly out of that
place.

I wrote to Mary begging her to bring Mick over, still
clinging to some romantic notion that he would sweep
Molly off her feet. Meantime, I started going home
regularly and always taking along a few special cakes
or a bunch of flowers. Mother had never been used to
such treats except on birthdays. At first my father was
huffy because he disapproved of educating girls and
even more of unmarried girls living away from home,
or so he said. I think he resented the fact that I had got
away. I realised rather late in the day that my mother
must have had to fight hard for me to be allowed to
stay and study in Ireland and so I was finally grateful
to her for the privilege and for the independence it
now allowed me.

Mary did bring Mick over to Edinburgh that New
Year and, despite father's protests I managed to get
Molly to come to the races at Powderhall. She and
Mick hit it off immediately as I always knew they
would, but father's hold over her was stronger than I

could understand and she wouldn't even invite Mick to the house, never mind agree to go out with him. But at least Mick was smitten and I hoped he could work it out from there. He did, of course, although in a dogged, roundabout way which I later came to know as part of his character. He enrolled on a course in counselling at a college in Edinburgh. This course wouldn't start till the following October, but in the meantime he had several weekends in Scotland looking for digs and "getting to know the lie of the land" as he so aptly put it. I don't think it was just the geography of the area he was finding out about. He stayed in a B&B quite near our house and started going to Mass in our chapel on the Sundays he was around. Father had started going back to Mass after years of non-attendance since he'd had the bad news from the hospital about the state of his arteries. Mick met father outside the church gates and chatted to him while they waited for his bus home. They made friends quite quickly and so it was father who actually invited Mick back to the house because he was eager for news of home and family and work colleagues left behind in Ireland.

The news was rarely good although I sensed that Mick played it down. There seemed to be a lot of burning and looting of shops. The supermarket just round the corner from Mick's parents' home had been bombed several times and it had become a standing joke in the community not to bother shopping but to wait and see what groceries landed in their gardens. The B Specials had been called up and Tony ("wee Fenian bastard" from our old village), whether driven to make his stance clear, or just in need of a job, joined up. Never the brightest of individuals, Tony had become an idiot when they gave him a gun. One night, patrolling the unapproved road from our village which led over the border he had been frightened by the sound of heavy breathing in a field he was passing. He had shouted, "Halt who goes there?" but no reply had come, just the same loud, regular breathing. He shouted again and there was still no reply, so he fired his Sten gun into the hedge. Next morning the farmer found his donkey shot dead in the field. Poor Tony became a laughing-stock in the village after that. Father and Mick had a good laugh about it too, but I shuddered at the thought of people with guns patrolling the lovely quiet roads of my childhood.

On fine days Mick and father did their talking outdoors as Mick would accompany him on his walks. Later that year they began to make day-trips here and there so that my father could show Mick Scotland. Although Molly was never invited along on these trips she reaped the benefit from them in the form of respite from my father's constant demands upon her and in having a much happier man to deal with when he came home cheerful afterwards. Father was soon as anxious as Molly for Mick's course to start. Although only noticeable to someone like myself who was observing it, Molly and Mick's courtship was coming on very nicely. When father was happily watching his favourite programmes after a day out, Molly would show Mick the garden or ask him to walk the dog with her because it was getting dark or she would need his advice about some broken household device. And only someone as self-absorbed as father could have failed to see the change in her face and bearing. There seems nothing as powerful as love in making people beautiful.

Very gradually they became more open about their feelings, but there was no exact point when any one could say the affair started and so father found himself accepting the situation as if it had always been a fact. Mick waited until he came over to start his course to ask father formally for Molly's hand.

They then became officially engaged and were to be married as soon as Mick finished his course in two years' time.

CHAPTER 8

"The summer's gone and all the flowers are dying."

Molly's happiness with Mick made me poignantly aware of my own longing for a boyfriend which had been so beautifully stilled for a while in my relationship with Pat Molloy. I used to wonder sometimes if perhaps there really was only one match for each of us and I had lost mine and would be doomed to a solitary life like an unlucky swan whose mate dies young. As the year wore on and their closeness grew I used to go off by myself to Aberdour and wander over the Hawkcraig with the dogs. Amongst the swards of harebells and wild scabious which reflected the blueness of the sea, the brambles were ripening and the spring-flowering bluebells were scattering their seeds purposefully amongst the tall bleached grass. The dogs would run wildly around the top of the cliff and stalk each other amongst the bracken, suddenly surprising each other with great yelps of delight in a tangled mass of coloured fur. They loved the exercise, the weather and the place. They were totally and unreservedly happy. I seemed to be the only creature there at odds with life. I felt somehow I was not where I belonged and I ached with longings that I barely understood. I had been reading Donne's poems and the line, "No man is an island," made me bitter. How wrong he was, I thought. I was an island. I was sure most people were islands because how could anybody, however willing, feel another's pain? And how could anybody love somebody as much as themselves? Sheer survival instinct dictated against it. Yet I had loved Uncle John like that. I would have laid down my life for him. And having found such love I would settle for the giving and taking of nothing less. But I was sure I would never find it in a world where everything was being de-emotionalised; where disasters like the bombings in Ireland made headline news and the grief of bereaved families prime viewing.

I had been out on dates with boys I met at university but it seemed as soon as they could find a quiet corner or get into a darkened cinema, they were only interested in groping me. This was the swinging sixties; the pill had arrived and many felt compelled to show their willingness to indulge in free love. I was a pretty "with it" teenager and I had never had reason to consider myself prim before, but I just wasn't interested in being groped by some guy I hardly knew. And I wasn't the only one. I had made a couple of really good friends who felt the same way. We had a lot of laughs but had decided that it was usually best to go home together after a party or a dance. So none of us had a boyfriend when "Operation Match" descended on the university in the spring to run a pilot scheme.

We thought it would be a hoot to try computer dating and agreed that it could hardly be any less successful than other avenues we'd tried.

To make it more fun we decided to create a fictional character made up of the features of all three of us and to share the dates -a minimum of six was guaranteed. We had a hilarious afternoon filling in the form for this fabulous creature who would bear little resemblance to any of us. "Height? Weight?" Eye colour? it asked. Since Emma was only four foot eleven and weighed about six stone and Morag was five foot ten and weighed at least twice that, we put down five foot seven and nine stone which was, in fact, about my size. Under "Eye colour" we wrote hazel since Emma's were green, Morag's a lovely dark brown and mine blue. And so on. We thought we should make the name humourous, but after a good deal of debate and some ludicrous names such as Anna Conda, Catherine Wheel and Ophelia Muscles, we settled on calling her my first name, Emma's second name and Morag's surname. She was briefly called Grainne Ainsley-Smith. But we all felt the Christian name Grainne too Irish to go with the surname, so I chose to call her, and later myself, Geraldine instead. We gave the address and telephone number of Edinburgh University Women's Union and posted it off. Over the next few days we had many giggles over how we were going to decide who got what date but, in the end, we decided to do it in the same order as the name. So I would get the first date. In the interests of personal safety we were to arrange to meet in a public place such as a café or a bar. The two not on the date were to turn up just before hand and sit at a discreet distance to eye up the subject. When the servitor announced the first phone call for Geraldine Ainsley-Smith over the Tannoy we didn't react for a second or two. Then, just as he started to repeat it we all squealed in unison and made for the phone. When it came to speaking, however, we realised that we hadn't rehearsed anything and I ended up with the receiver while the other two giggled. I don't know why my Claire Bloom accent emerged at that point, but I found myself speaking in a really plummy voice which sent the other two into a state of apoplexy with stifled laughter. I arranged to meet him next evening at Potter's bar, his choice of venue, which was only a few hundred yards from the Union. After all the hysteria leading up to the first date the actual meeting was very disappointing. He had said he was a member of a gliding club and I thought he'd be an all-action man. But, in fact, he was all mouth. He told me all about himself, from the moment of conception almost and he was so boring I found myself yawning over the first drink, which I had been nursing for ages. The last thing I wanted to do was get tipsy with a guy like this in tow. God only knows what I might have said or done. I kept signing behind his back to the other two who were sitting in a corner to come and join us in the hope that they might liven up the conversation. But they shook their heads and would have allowed me to fry if I hadn't jumped up suddenly as if I'd just seen them and said,

"Oh, there's some friends of mine over there, let's join them," and pounced on their table before they could escape. Try as they might they couldn't get a decent conversation out of the guy either. It was all, "And my mother said that I was the bravest little chap...." and "I was the lead soprano in our church choir..."and stuff like that out of him. Eventually Emma said in a sweet voice which put Morag and I on red alert, "Do you live alone now?"

"Yes," he replied and was just about to plunge into a long explanation when she him stopped him in his tracks.

"No wonder," she said, "You're so bloody boring."
I grabbed her by the arm and dragged her out of the bar before she said any more. We had a fit of the giggles when we got outside and careered down Potter's Row pretending to be gliders. We reckoned he didn't need a glider he was so stiff-necked. He probably just launched himself off the top of Arthur's Seat and glided on the thermals.

The next date, which was Emma's, was very successful. She met a bloke who was studying at the Royal Dick Veterinary College. They met at Deacon Brodies Bar where all the vet students hung out. Morag and I felt a bit incongruous there but when we tried to crash in on Emma's date she gave us the evil eye. She had really hit it off with him and wanted us to skedaddle. So we did, that's what friends do.

Emma actually married the vet bloke in her final year so we reckon the computer was able to work something out of the data we'd given it.

Morag's date was worse than mine. He was a nightmare of a medical student, prematurely balding with badly fitting false teeth and a personality to go with them. Emma and I tittered in the corner of Potter's bar, which we have studiously avoided since. We decided the men who chose this as a rendezvous were severely lacking in imagination and probably everything else. Morag was struggling to get a word out of this bloke and kept signing to us to come and join her. We let her stew. It was such a laugh watching them. When we saw her get up and move towards our table we shot off to the ladies. She came rushing in behind us and tried to persuade us to join them.

"No way," said Emma. "Send Frankenstein home."

"He won't bloody go," said Morag. "He's a zombie. I've tried hinting and then I tried insulting him, but he just sits there hiding behind those enormous china teeth."

"There's only one thing for it then," I said in a melodramatic voice. "We've got to make a run for it."

"The window," hissed Emma, playing the part. And before we could blink an eye she was climbing into the washbasin and out of the tiny window. This is not such a difficult task if you're a four-foot pigmy and weigh only six stones. It was considerably harder for Morag and I and we were rather hot and dishevelled when we finally struggled through and landed on the street, with stockings shredded, to the amazement of passers-by. We were unfit to move for about ten minutes we were so paralysed with laughter and for hours afterwards, every time we thought of

the bloke sitting waiting for our return from the
Ladies we were seized with the giggles again.

The next date was mine and the others after that I
handed over to Morag because they were of no
consequence to me. I thought I had found the man of
my dreams.
He had arranged to pick me up at the Bus Station in
St. Andrew's Square because I was out of town
spending a weekend at home. He asked how he would
recognise me and I gave him a detailed description of
what I looked like and what I'd be wearing. Then I
asked him the same question and he simply said he'd
be wearing a daffodil in his buttonhole. And so I
stood like a prize idiot in the Bus Station in St
Andrew's Square in Edinburgh, looking at the
buttonhole of every man who wore a jacket.
Suddenly my view was blocked. I realised with a start
that I was looking into a vast expanse of checked shirt
which was so close to me that I could smell its line-
dried freshness. I looked up slowly and timidly into
his face. I caught sight of dark chest hair at the open
neck just before I spotted the daffodil sticking out of
his shirt pocket. His eyes were wide and grey-green in
colour and had a sardonic look that made me quiver.
He had a mop of poker-straight black hair and a big
open smile of perfect strong white teeth. I suddenly
felt very shy and dropped my eyes to his feet. At the
end of an incredibly long pair of blue-denimed legs I
saw the biggest pair of desert boots I've ever seen in
my life.
    "Come on then, Geraldine, let's give it a
whirl," he said in a thrilling voice and took my arm
and led me out of the bus station. He had parked his
car in the square and when my two friends, who were
tailing me, saw that I intended to get into it they set up
such a fit of coughing that I was forced to turn round.
I think Morag was just about to throw a fake fit in

order to get our attention. I gave them a "push off"
look which they ignored. I intended to get in quickly
and shut the car door and vroom off and leave them
there. But it was not that kind of car. It was an ancient
Jowett Javelin which I preferred instantly to the shiny
BMW that it stood next to. He fiddled a bit with the
key before it would let him in and then he leaned over
and unlocked the passenger door. Just as I was about
to open it he said, "Wait," and came round to my side
to open it for me. Then, mock grandly, he handed me
in like a princess and shut the door. He then climbed
in the driver's door and slammed it shut. The
passenger door fell right off into the road, exposing
nearly all of my very long legs to any Edinburgh
shopper who cared to look. They appeared to be clad
only in white lacy tights since my mini-skirt had
virtually disappeared when I sat down. Emma and
Morag seized the opportunity to talk to me while he
tied on the passenger door with a piece of rope,
obviously carried for such emergencies.

"Excuse me, have you got change for the
parking meter?" Emma said this loudly while Morag
hissed under her breath

"You shouldn't go in a car with a strange
man."

"No, I'm sorry, I can't help you," I was saying
when I saw Morag preparing to throw one of her
pretend fits again. She was very good at this and I
knew if she did it we'd end up taking her to hospital
and hanging around casualty all afternoon if she felt
bloody-minded enough. So, I gave in.

"Meet my friends," I said through clenched
teeth. He roared with laughter.

"Can I give you a lift anywhere, girls?" he
asked, not the least bit bothered by them crashing in
on our date.

"We'll go wherever you're going," said Morag
determinedly and I thought she probably fancies him

too. And I was right. I gave her a withering look, but she pretended not to notice.

"I was going to dine at the Staff Club," he said matter-of-factly. "You're welcome to come along if you like."

"Thank you, that would be very nice," replied Morag despite another withering look from me and a dig in the ribs from Emma's very bony elbow.

And so I spent my first date with Ian with that pair twittering in the background. The Staff Club was very posh with a restaurant where the tables were beautifully laid with white cloths, candles and silverware. It could have been so romantic for two. The waiter raised his eyebrows just a fraction as he pulled out our chairs and seated three adoring teenage girls round a member of staff whom he probably knew at least by sight.

"I hope we're not going to ruin your reputation," said Emma in a very sexy voice.

"I hope you are," he replied with a pretend leer.

At this point Morag turned her big spaniel eyes on him and fluttered her long dark lashes in such a teasing way that I decided it was time to get rid of the pair of them. Thinking the direct approach would be best, I stood up and said, "Let's go to the powder room girls," in the manner of the sheriff in cowboy films inviting outlaws to a draw.

Emma stood up immediately, but Morag hesitated, realising, no doubt that she could have him all to herself, crafty bitch.

But Emma grabbed her arm, saying, "Your nose is shiny, Morag. It definitely needs a spot of powder."

Or a punch, I thought.

When we got to the no-man's-land of the ladies I said simply, "Bugger off, you two. It's my date."

"Fairy nuff." said Emma.

"No way," said Morag who was fast becoming my ex-friend. Again I thought briefly of punching her on the nose, but realised we might end up in casualty after all.

So instead I said, "Hands off then, he's mine!"

"We'll see," said Morag. I could see there was no point in continuing the discussion and decided I'd just have to charm him more than her.

And so we all had dinner together for which he had to pay since we were penniless students and he was a gentleman. He took it all in good part and said that he reckoned he ought to pay for three since he had foolishly assumed that Geraldine Ainsley-Smith was only one person and so it was his mistake. (Morag had blurted out the whole story of our combined name as soon as she'd swallowed one glass of wine.) Afterwards we repaired upstairs to the games room where we almost gave the staff heart-attacks as we tried to play pool, threatening to accidentally rip up the green baize on several occasions. Our attempts at table-tennis were no better, especially since the wine had gone straight to our heads. In fact this was the first time I had ever had more than one glass of alcohol. It was taboo in our house because of my father's drinking. The table tennis balls seemed to have a life of their own and were whizzing round the room like small plastic comets in a toy factory. I tried apologising to the handsome giant for creating such havoc in his sedate club but he said he was really enjoying it and it was time somebody put a bit of life in the joint. After that I had a great time. The wine had made me very mellow and forgiving and I was really glad that my friends were enjoying the evening with me.

After that we all spent many happy days together in Ian's company. There were days on Cramond Island when we walked out across the causeway at low tide and picnicked and swam and dashed back across the causeway just before it was covered by the in-coming sea. There were climbs up Arthur's Seat where Ian played his fiddle at the top and we all danced. There were soirees at his flat when his band practised there. But there were no more trips to the Staff Club.

Only I went there with him. For, from the time of that first meal, I was undisputedly his girlfriend and we spent romantic times together without the others.

Quite soon I was seeing him about five times a week. He had become an essential part of my life. Often we just drove out together in one of his ancient cars. He had a couple of Bristols as well as the Javelin. Often I would sing as we cruised along, mostly haunting Irish airs which he loved. My favourite was She Moved Through The Fair. He liked it too because the words and tune are very lovely, but he liked it even more, I suspect, because the marriage of the lovers never takes place. The more I got to know Ian, the more I realised that he was a complete misogamist who considered marriage to be a trap devised by women for the ensnarement of men. This explained why such a handsome, good-humoured guy was still single and fancy-free at the age of twenty-eight. But, since I was just finishing my first year at university and had three years more to go, his distaste for marriage quite suited me at that moment in time.

We'd been going out for several months when I brought him to Fife to meet my parents, on mother's insistence. Afterwards we went for a meal in Kirkcaldy. We were driving along the promenade just as the sun was setting on the water and it was so beautiful I wanted to swim there. I said, "Stop!" so loudly that Ian did just that and the car behind almost ran into him. When I explained I just wanted to swim off the prom he was a bit annoyed at first and said I was being ridiculous and the beach was more sea-coal than sand. But when I started stripping off into my underwear he decided to join me and we swam off together into a rose-tinted sea. When we came out of the water we had to run up and down the beach to get dry as we had no towel. It was wonderfully invigorating, feeling the sea breeze ruffle the droplets of water on my body and the hairs on my arms stand on end with the chill and hearing the beating of my heart in unison with my feet as I pounded along the wet sand. We were breathless and panting when we decided to get dressed. We had to put on our outer clothes without any underwear as we had used that to swim in. I turned away from him as I sat in the back seat struggling out of my wet things and into my dress which clung to every inch of my body on the way down. And I hoped that mother would never find out that I had taken my clothes off in front of a man. I was nineteen but I had very little experience of men and I was bounded by the teachings of my mother and the Catholic Church which were much the same thing. We went to the restaurant as planned. A lovely glow suffused my body from the cold water and the exercise. My skin was smooth and rosy as carnelian, polished in the palm for aeons and I was pleasantly aware of my nakedness under my thin summer dress. My tingling erect nipples gently rubbed against the soft cotton of my dress as I raised my arms to eat and drink or sleek back my damp hair which fell round my face touching my lips with the salty taste of the sea. I ate like a horse because the swim and the run had made me work up an appetite. Ian, on the other hand, picked at his food, moving it around his plate, but eating very little. I asked if he wanted something else and he gave a low sardonic laugh that I did not understand at the time. He didn't want to dally in the restaurant although we sometimes quite liked to do so, but was eager to be going. In the car he asked me if I really had to stay with my parents that night and I told him my mother was expecting me. After that we drove in brooding silence. When I was leaving him at the door he held me very firmly by the shoulders, pulled me close so that I felt him hard and urgent against me and kissed me with a passion I didn't think he possessed. Then he asked in a strangely hoarse voice if I definitely had to stay. When I nodded he turned on his heel and left. I dreamt about him all night and awoke feeling more hopeful and happy than I had done for a long time, thinking maybe I was going to get a second chance at love.

The next day, which was a Sunday, he arrived bright and early to take me for a drive. I was just getting my things together when mother asked where I was going. I looked at Ian.

"Perth, perhaps," he said. She eyed him for a moment and he looked away. I thought she was going to suggest she come along for the ride and was cringing inwardly, but what she did say surprised me more.

"We're just about to go to Mass. You might as well come with us. It'll save you hanging about waiting for her."

I think he was dumbstruck. He never went to church, any church. He just nodded and said, "I'll give you a lift if you like." And so Ian came to church and was bored out of his skull. Afterwards he said, "You don't believe all that mumbo-jumbo, do you?" I did but I felt that was not what he wanted to hear so I didn't reply.

We dropped my parents off and drove away into the hills and the sunshine for the rest of the day. The road from Dunfermline to Perth must be one of the most scenic in Britain and soon we settled back comfortably to enjoy the ever-changing view of hills and forests. Even the verges at the roadside were beautiful where great swathes of big white dog daisies and splashes of pink and purple lupins added vivid colour to the tall waving summer grasses. I begged

Ian to stop before Perth in the little village of
Luncarty where the dog daisies and lupins were
augmented by fabulous Turkish poppies in vibrant
shades of scarlet and orange, their shimmering cups
brimming with sun. To my delight, I found delicate
pink ones too with dainty picot edges and dusky
interiors. I wanted to gather armfuls of these but Ian
stopped me, reminding me that they would be wilted
long before we got home and consoling me with the
promise that we would come back another day and
dig up a root so that I could look on them every
summer in my own garden. But we never did.

We drove past Luncarty into open country to find a
quiet place to have our picnic lunch. We chose a
secret spot in a tiny dell, running down to the banks of
a stream. Ian had brought a wicker hamper with real
cutlery and proper plates and glasses just like a
movie. There was a delicious cold platter and a really
smooth red wine. Ian had only one glass because he
was driving, but I finished the bottle eventually
because it tasted so good to eat and drink in the fresh
air. I started running around and doing somersaults,
full of high spirits. There was a lovely big patch of
ragged robin, one of my favourite flowers, just down
by the stream. It was the sight of the expanse of pink
from the road that had made me want to stop there so
that I could run through it barefoot. After the third
glass of wine I threw off my shoes and ran skipping
and dancing amongst the flowers. Ian sat bemused on
the picnic rug watching me and I began to play to the
gallery, throwing in a few high kicks and handstands,
showing off my knickers without a second thought.

"Come dance with me," I laughed. But he
shook his head. I tried to pull him up by the hands but
he was enormous and unmovable. I rumpled his hair
and stuck flowers behind his ears. My heart was
pounding so hard from the running around that I'm
sure he could hear it. Suddenly he grabbed me and

pulled me down on top of him and kissed me as he had done on the doorstep the night before. The world began to spin and all sorts of new sensations surged in my head so that I felt quite dizzy. The whole world disappeared and there was only this moment and this man. I felt his tongue in my mouth, a totally new and exciting sensation for me, and I relaxed and allowed him to roll me onto the grass. He began to nibble my neck and I became pliant as the blossom that I lay on. Even when he began stroking my breasts I yielded, my amber nipples reaching up to make contact with his skin, with his mouth with every inch of his body, despite a fleeting thought about what my mother might say. It was only the tantalising, forbidden touch of his cool fingers inside my pants that forced me to try and focus on what was happening. But I felt drugged with powerful new sensations and my mind battled with my body while the caressing continued to sedate both.. I wanted to stay like that forever and ever but I knew I musn't. Then Ian fumbled with his zip. He revealed himself naked and erect and tried to replace his fingers with his red, swollen penis. I had never seen a man like that before. It was disgusting. I sat bolt upright.

"Get off," I screamed and pushed him away.

"What's wrong?" he asked. "First time?"

"We're not married. We shouldn't be doing this!"

"Don't be such a silly-Billy," he said. "that doesn't matter."

"It does to me. I can't do it. It's wrong."

"You don't really believe all that old cock, surely?

"I believe in decency, if that's what you mean," I said in an angry voice to hide my feelings of stupidity and shame.

"Come on, I'll look after you. It's the most natural thing in the world. He took a condom from his pocket.

"I said NO. Which letter are you having difficulty with, the "N" or the "O"?

"You're a bloody teaser," he said, tucking himself in furiously.

I bolted then, not knowing what to say or how to explain. I wasn't even sure that I could explain what I felt. I just kept running and running till I sank down exhausted and sobbing in the long cool grass.

After a while I heard Ian calling my name, but didn't answer, at a loss as to how I was going to face him now that we had seen each other almost naked. Everything had changed between us so how were we ever going to manage the long journey home together? He came upon me still lying crying and knelt down beside me.

"Come on," he said quite gently, but it was the voice one might use to a child rather than a lover. I couldn't bear to look at him so I didn't move. He picked me up firmly in his enormous arms and carried me back to the car. We scarcely spoke till we got to my door where he dropped me with a brusque "good night" and then drove off with a great burst of acceleration into the evening. I went to bed and cried. Molly noticed I was upset and came to my room as soon as her duties to father would allow her. She coaxed me to tell her what was wrong and eventually, with a good deal of misgiving because sex was always a taboo subject in our house, I told her. She was nine years older than me, the same age as Ian, in fact, and I felt I could trust her judgement. In effect, she said exactly what mother would have said, on the rare occasions that she had broached such a topic. In a nutshell it was, "if a man respects you he will wait." She advised me to write to Ian stating this position. I

94

got a reply by return of post. It began without endearment:

Geraldine,

Look you'd better get yourself sorted in a hurry because I'm fed up playing stop-go and I'm fed up playing the villain and I've had enough of writhing around amongst steering wheels and stairheads and backyards. Makeup your mind what you're trying to achieve and you might get some cooperation. You've convinced me that essential chastity is meaningful to you but you've convinced me of nothing else. If existing limitations are acceptable for Christ's accept them and stop fooling yourself that there is any virtue in discomfort and restrictive practices because all that comes of it is estrangement and mistrust and frustration.

Ian

It was the late sixties and I thought I was probably the only virgin left in Europe But I felt trapped by my family and my religion. I raged against Ian, against God and against my own feelings but I didn't see him again. Yet I secretly hankered after him for years. Often that swollen, red member would figure in my dreams, at once repelling and enticing me, scaring me yet inviting my touch. I would wake ashamed of these dreams and wonder if I was a bad person, believing what mother said that god punished women for having sex with the terrible pains of childbirth. This caused me great doubts about the justness of God because I knew mother suffered enough in the act of sex itself.

When I was still quite a young child I got up one night, unable to sleep because of the heat of the bed which I shared with two older sisters, I had wriggled out from between them and was crouched on the cool lino floor with my back against the bedroom wall. This wall separated our room from the livingroom. In

95

the silence of the night I heard moaning and then the whistling of a cane. I knew that sound well as father often beat us with a springy bamboo cane that brought us up in big red weals and sometimes cut us. We used to compare the marks in the secrecy of the outside loo. We didn't dare even whisper about them in the house for fear of attracting his attention and getting more of the same. The sound of the cane came again and again and the moaning was stifled as if the person being beaten was trying not to make a noise. I opened the bedroom door a tiny crack and peeped through. I saw my mother being driven round and round the livingroom on all fours like a heifer at an auction. She was completely naked and my father was raining blows on her back and buttocks with all his strength. I felt a scream rising in my throat but swallowed it because I was so scared he would hear me. Silently I crept under the big iron bedstead into the farthest corner where I knew my father could not reach.

I woke up in bed next morning unsure whether I had actually witnessed or just dreamt about the horrible scene from the night before. I watched mother carefully for signs but she was very attentive to my father as usual and betrayed nothing in her movements. But then we children all did the same after we had had a beating. Whinging was forbidden in our family. I now wonder if any of my sisters knew these terrible things too and, like me, were scared to speak about them. I suppose if we didn't talk about them, they hadn't really happened.

The incident with Ian brought back these ugly memories of childhood which I had almost managed to forget. I became quite withdrawn, turning them over and over in my mind, trying to make sense of them. I was back home for the summer vacation from university and could hardly bear to be in the same room as my father again.

I was truly grateful, therefore, when my mother's sister wrote to say that she had acquired a holiday home in Donegal and any of us girls would be welcome there over the summer. I decided to go for the rest of the holidays despite all the stories about my aunt. I needed the change and she needed some help to put the house to rights. It had been lying empty for seventeen years since her uncle and his family had emigrated to America. She had let it over the winter to divers who were salvaging a wreck off Fanad Head, but she had little hope that they would have done anything in the way of improvements. It was with a sense of relief, then, that I packed my bags and set off for Ireland again. Even Molly's parting words, "Rather you than me," didn't put me off.

When Molly had contacted impetigo as a child she had gone to live with Aunt Roisin for a time so that she would not infect the other children in the family. She told me my aunt's voice when angry was as terrifying as a banshee and her sarcasm was so sharp it could flay the hide of an elephant. Fortunately for Molly my aunt mostly employed these talents to promote the misery of little boys. She had a famous saying,

"When you meet a little boy always box his ears. If he's not coming out of trouble, he's just going into it."

All my childhood days I was grateful that I was not a little boy. My mother confessed to the same feeling. It was definitely better being Aunt Roisin's sister than her brother my mum said because she could climb higher, spit further and fight dirtier than any boy. All of which was good if you were a girl and she was on your side. Pretty bad if you were a boy though, especially since she was lovely looking. Roisin is an Irish name meaning black rose and was, by all accounts, very appropriate for my aunt who had the fair complexion and raven hair of the traditional colleen. Her eyes I knew from first hand, they were startlingly blue and inscrutable. I thought the eyes of God might look a bit like that.

She wasn't a big woman but her presence was always felt in any room. It was felt on the camogy pitch too, according to the stories. Aunt Roisin was a skilled and fierce devotee of the game and is reputed to have played on in a desperately fought college final despite having her nose broken by a camogy stick in the first ten minutes. In that at least I felt I could understand her through my own love of fast rough games.

CHAPTER 9

"From glen to glen and down the mountainside."

My aunt met me off the ferry at Belfast. I was
surprised by how ordinary she looked amongst the
crowd of people waiting on the quayside. Seeing her
standing there in slacks and anorak, it was hard to
believe the stories my mother had told me about her
over the years. I was sure they had gained a bit in
glamour and daring in the telling and the passage of
time. I hadn't seen her for about ten years but before
we left Belfast Harbour in the car, I had reason to
remember her legendary lack of driving skills. The
RUC man in flak jacket and Sten gun, who was
directing the traffic, jumped aside as she performed an
emergency stop. She wasn't expecting traffic control
and was going too fast. Once on the open road she
roared off like Stirling Moss and I just prayed silently
while she chatted away in between cursing slow
drivers and over-taking anything that appeared in
front of her. She really put the boot down on the
climb up through Glenshane Pass, consigning all
other vehicles to the crawler lane. At the top of the
pass there were boxes scattered as if they had fallen
off a lorry and a man at the side of the road was
frantically trying to flag us down. My aunt almost ran
him over and drove through the boxes, scattering
them even further. I was dreading what might happen
at the border. But the officers on duty at both the
British and Irish Customs Posts seemed to know her
and just waved her on.
And so, only about two hours after leaving the ferry,
we arrived in the small village of Portsalon where the
ramshackle little cottage stood blissfully unaware of
the hurricane personality that was about to take it in
hand. I was grateful to get my feet on firm ground

again. Any bit of ground would've done, but she had brought me to the Garden of Eden. From the doorstep of the cottage the hedges of wild fushia stretched as far as the eye could see, snaking their brilliant red and purple pathway round bends in the road to the shores of the Atlantic. The peat bogs were frothy with scented meadow sweet and clumps of pink mallow bloomed amongst a scatter of rounded dove-coloured pebbles at the front of the house. Below us gleamed the whole two-mile sweep of Ballymacstocker Strand. One of the most beautiful beaches in the world, it is bordered by clear bright water and enfolded by soft green hills. The tide was out and a light aircraft seemed to be practising take-offs and landings on the long, smooth stretch of golden shore.

There were no people on the strand and I was glad. As a child my family had had this beach almost entirely to themselves most summers. This was where my mother and her mother and her mother's mother came from and it seemed to be known only to such as us. I had been worried that in my absence the world might have found it. But I needn't have worried about the tourists. Cheap tickets to Spain and the Troubles kept them all away. The people to worry about were much nearer home.

I stood there in the healing evening and allowed the beauty of the wilderness to overwhelm me. Standing there I understood why my aunt had come home to retire here after a lifetime's travelling and why she had bought this tumbledown cottage years earlier in preparation for this time.

"It's a fool's paradise," she said, breaking in on my thoughts, "and old fools are the worst of fools. Come on, we can't stand here all night. Let's brave the ghosts of the old house."

I looked at her questioningly as we turned to enter the dim hallway.

"My Uncle Johnny died here, you know, alone in an alcoholic stupor. His wife and children were in America. He couldn't stand it over there and had come home. Aye, this place draws its children back as surely as the moon draws the tides."

A shiver of foreboding crawled down my spine. She flicked the old brown bakelite switch beside the door but nothing happened. We moved further into the gloom and tried the light in the livingroom. It didn't work either.

"Must be a fuse," she said in a calm voice as I felt panic well up inside me. For, although it was a fine summer's evening outdoors, the house was dank and full of shadows. It was surrounded on three sides by hills, barren, stony hills soaked in the sweat and memories of the people they had broken. Suddenly I tripped over and fell on top of a stinking, slimy thing that yielded to my weight and felt cold and clammy to the touch. I couldn't get up because I was slipping about on it and I couldn't even cry out because I was rigid with fear. But a small whimper of terror must have escaped my lips.

"Get up, you silly bitch," said my aunt, yanking me by the arm. "It's only an old oilskin those untidy blackguards have left lying about. Look at the state of this place. Just wait till I get my hands on them."

My eyes, adjusting to the gloom, began to pick out the messiest living quarters I had ever seen. The house had been leased to the divers over the previous six months and they had certainly made themselves at home. They were supposed to have vacated the premises by now but it was obvious from the used cups at the sides of chairs and the personal belongings lying around that they had not done so.

"Sit down," she commanded, "in case you fall over something else. I'll find the fuse box and sort out the fault."

I did as I was told and she slipped off into the gloom. There was a lot of banging of drawers and cupboard doors as she searched in the kitchen for matches and a candle. This was followed by a horrible scraping sound of chair legs across a flagstone floor and then, a small flicker of light. Next came a banshee wail which stopped my heart again.

"The electric's been cut off, the blackguards!"

"What'll we do?" I asked lamely.

"Hold the candle and I'll see if I can reconnect it."

"Isn't that's illegal?" I began before her withering look silenced me.

"Go and look for a screwdriver or even a flat-bladed knife will do," she said, thrusting the candle into my hand.

"You could electrocute yourself."

"A screwdriver!" she commanded and, against all my instincts and safety lessons, I went and got a knife and then held the candle while she poked about with the wires. I half expected to see her light up like Lundy when the match is put to the bonfire.
Minutes later the lights in the house were blazing as my aunt shot from room to room surveying the mess. A barnacle-covered ship's wheel lay on the kitchen floor and one or two pieces of shiny brass glittered on the table. They stood on newspapers and had obviously been recently cleaned with the Brasso and fine steel wool lying beside them.

"Seems they found something on the wreck at any rate," sniffed my aunt, but I doubt there's enough here to pay the electricity bill, never mind the rent they owe."
So saying, she picked up the objects and took them out to her car while I stood staring at her in disbelief.

"Make yourself useful," she said, "Come and get clean bedding from the car. Make up a couple of beds for us."

I followed her without a word. She piled sheets, pillows and downies into my arms.

"The front room upstairs has the best view," she said.

I didn't move, terrified of going up there. She must have realised this because she took back some of the bedding and went up the narrow wooden stairs ahead of me.

"Never be scared of ghosts." she said quite softly. "It's the living you have to look out for."

I shivered with dread and wished I'd never come back.

Then suddenly the dark stair arrived at a bright room with windows looking out across the flower-filled peat bogs falling away to the wide sweep of Lough Swilly below. To the east the dark shape of Carablah with its secret lake was already casting long shadows. But in the west the setting sun was anointing the heads of the Knockalla Hills and pouring its blessing warmly at their feet where they dipped into the rosy sea at Warden Sands.

The room, despite the ravages of time and the mess made by the divers, was lovely. I had heard about it often in my mother's stories, but nothing had prepared me for what I saw. To enter there was like changing worlds. Downstairs there was an ancient Donegal cottage with turf fire and dark smoky interior. Upstairs I found myself in a gypsy caravan. The wood-clad walls curved inwards towards the top where they met the wooden ceiling and where they joined a pattern of shamrocks and harps had been hand carved all the way round. A small press with fancy doors in coloured glass had been built into these walls and at the top of the stair two tiny rooms, also with quaint glass doors, had been sectioned off the main area. The last shafts of sunlight filtered through the windows, touching the walls with gold and spilling little gems of red and blue light on the floor.

103

Standing there, even in the fading daylight, I could imagine myself a Romany on the open road. This effect must have been greatly heightened on a windy night with the clouds scudding past the moon.

"Sure he was a daft old eejit," said my aunt, noticing my admiring glances. "Spent years doing this, and for what? To die in that dark hole downstairs because he was too drunk to get up here."
But I could tell by her voice that she had loved him. I moved to put my arm around her but she moved away and was suddenly flippant.

"See this?" She pointed to a small door in the section of wall that jutted out over the stair. "It's a coffin hatch. He realised that if he died up here they'd never get him down. So he made this. Thought of everything did Johnny ... except maybe dying alone."
I shuddered and she said no more. We went downstairs because my aunt decided to put the car round the back and I went out with her into the twilight. My heart sank as I heard her curse loudly again.

"Come and see this," she shouted, "those blackguards have no intention of moving."
The ground behind the house where Aunt Roisin intended to grow palm trees and other exotic plants in her retirement was piled high with rubbish. There were mountains of empty cans, piles of plastic and glass bottles and a stack of six-months' ash from the fire. There was a storage tank full of paraffin and a huge pile of kindling next to the turf stack. A big old Mercedes stood next to the stack and further up the hillside lay a fibreglass dingy. The outboard motor for this and a Jerry-can of petrol had been carelessly dumped at the back door.

I'll never know why she did it. Maybe the threat to her cherished dream made her see red. But before I could stop her she had sloshed paraffin all over the dinghy and thrown a match. Bright tongues of flame leapt high into the evening sky, rapidly devouring the boat and lighting up the hillside.

"Don't stand there gawping," she said, "run down to Dunleavy's where that lot are drinking and tell them to look up the hill. Tell them they'll see their boat burning and if they don't get up here quick with the money they owe the car's the next thing to burn." I knew she meant it and took to my heels down the Bog Road. It was at least a mile to the pub and I wondered how long she'd be prepared to wait in that mood.

I was about half way down the winding road on the blind side of a bend, keeping close to the hedge when I heard gruff, angry voices in the still air. Instinctively, I dived for cover.

"It'll be the old woman, let me handle it," said a soft Donegal voice.

"Pat was to take care of her on the road. It can't be her," said a Northern voice.

"He probably missed her. There's probably a simple explanation."

"They're onto us, I tell you, John-James. We should clear out while we've got the chance." This came in the harsh Northern accent.

"And leave all that stuff we've slaved to bring in? You must be joking."

" Where's that jerk, Pat, anyway? He should be here by now." The Northern voice sounded tetchy.

"Tell you what," said John-James, "I'll slip up to the house and sniff about. And stop worrying. Even Sherlock Holmes couldn't find the stuff we've hidden in there."

"Aye, you're right enough there, that old hatch is an amazing hidey-hole."

" So you stay on the roadside and keep a look-out for Pat. I'll just check out the old place. Give me the usual signal if you need me."

I held my breath as they passed within a foot of me. Then I hurried back up the hill on the inside of the hedge and slipped through a gap to hide behind the turf stack. A faint rustle of clothing and a strong smell of tobacco told me that the man called John-James was also watching the house from the back. My aunt was banging around in the kitchen, presumably preparing a meal, totally unaware of the noose of tension that surrounded her and the strangers skulking in the shadows.

Suddenly the back door opened and a basinful of water and potato peelings was flung out. John-James swore as they hit his face. I froze, but my aunt seemed not to have heard. Or maybe she had, for minutes later she walked out the front door with her coat on, got into her car and drove off. I didn't dare move but the Northern man came round to speak to John-James almost as soon as she left.

"Jesus, I can't believe it!" said the Northerner.

"I told you it'd be the old woman," said John-James.

"We'd better nip in and move the stuff."

"But what if she comes back?"

The Northern man mimed a knife slitting a throat.

"Jesus, you wouldn't do that, would you?"

"Curiosity killed the cat," said the other sardonically.

"You can count me out of that," said John-James. "Gun-running's one thing, murder's another."

"And what do you think people do with the guns we sell them?"

They went into the house together and shut the door and I heard no more of this conversation. They seemed to be in the livingroom so I crept round to the front of the building and peered in the window. I had just time to catch sight of the murky interior when the curtains were roughly drawn. So I pressed my ear to the wall. There was an eerie creaking and rending of wood and low voices. Desperate to hear what they were saying, I clung to the wall like ivy, all senses closed down except my hearing.

"Don't move or you're dead." The whisper almost burst my eardrums so intently had I been listening. The hand that covered my mouth was rough and salty, yet strangely familiar. I turned round and came face to face with Pat Molloy. I don't know which of us was more surprised.

"What are you doing here?" we whispered together and it would've been funny if the situation hadn't been so serious.

"You've got to get out of here," said Pat giving me a gentle shove. "And tell nobody what you've seen."

"But my aunt might come back," I said.

"Your aunt? Oh, Jesus, the old biddy's your aunt! Pat hesitated, "I'll look out for her."
Just then, as he was propelling me away from the house, headlights appeared at the bottom of the road and I recognised the sound of my aunt's big diesel. The Garda were behind her.

"Shit!" said Pat. "Now what?"

"Clear off or you'll get caught," I said.

"But they're desperate men, there's no saying what they'll do."

"Go!" I said, shaking him off.

"They're gun-runners, for God's sake…"

"I'll be OK." I said, pushing him face down in the ditch just as the car's headlights came round the final bend and lit up the whole countryside. I was torn between my desire to stop Pat getting caught and my desire to save my aunt from the murderous John-James. Fortunately, I'm a quick learner.

"Got any matches?" I asked fumbling in his pockets and removing some even as I spoke. I ran to the back door, poured petrol from the can under the paraffin tank, dropped a lighted match in the spillage and dived for cover. There was a terrific explosion which blew the windows out of the house and the car. The two men burst out, and seeing the Garda approach, made off on foot up the hill at the back of the house. My aunt and the Garda screeched to a halt, almost crashing into each other. The fire needed all their attention.

"Save my house!" she was shouting. "Never mind the blackguards." She grabbed a shovel and started throwing ash from the pile at the door on top of the blaze. The Garda followed suit and Pat had time to disappear into the darkness while I crept out of the hedge. A minute or two later I started to run towards the house as if I was just returning from Dunleavy's.

"You didn't give them much time," I said to my aunt as I ran round to the back of the house.

"Eejit," she said, "I didn't do this! Find a spade and start shovelling."
When the panic had died down, the house was thoroughly searched and the guns they had been hiding in the coffin hatch were confiscated. The Garda then set to asking my aunt and I many, many questions. She knew very little and I said I knew nothing. She couldn't describe the men since all communication with them had been by letter and I said I couldn't describe them because I hadn't delivered her message, that I had been too scared and had just sat in the hedge half way down the road till I had heard the explosion.
A search was mounted in the hills but I was pretty sure it would be unsuccessful. While we were busy fighting the fire I had observed a small plane land

briefly on the beach below and take off again into the night. I reckoned it had picked up passengers.

It was very late before my aunt and I finally got to bed. The house was uninhabitable and the nearest hotel was about twenty miles away. Aunt Roisin was very chatty on the journey, enjoying her part in the night's adventures, speculating wildly about the reason for the fire.

"To think they were using my house to hide guns, the blackguards. If I'd known that I'd have burnt their damn car too. They'd better not show their faces here again."

She didn't seem the least bit bothered that the house had been half-wrecked. She was sure the insurance would more than pay for it and she could get it rewired and re-plumbed to a much higher standard, not to mention complete redecoration and refurbishment. "You know," she said laughing, "those blackguards did me a favour!"

Her laugh echoed and reverberated round and round the listening hills. She was so pleased that I half wished I could admit my responsibility and get some of the praise. But there was no way I could ever reveal anything about what I knew. Noticing my silence, she mistook it for shock and was very solicitous. But I couldn't trust myself to speak in case I gave anything away. I tossed all night dreaming and waking fitfully, wondering if Pat was all right and where he was and whether I would ever see him again.

CHAPTER 10

"'The summer's gone and all the flowers are dying

"

After the dramatic start our holiday in Ireland settled into a much tamer affair. The house needed to be completely gutted and refurbished. Clearing up the debris took up so much of my time and energy in the days after the traumatic events that I hardly thought about them. I certainly never gave any serious consideration to Pat's role in the affair. And, if finding men in this remote spot of Donegal who where seriously interested in such work was a hard task, getting them to turn up when they said they would was even harder. Now I understood the witticism that if the Dutch lived in Ireland it would be the richest agricultural country in the world and if the Irish lived in Holland they would all drown. During the hours spent waiting for tradesmen my aunt and I made a virtue of necessity and lounged about planning the garden-to-be and ambled in the foothills which gave us a view of people coming for miles. But, it was a most relaxing time once we got over the urgency of things needing done. We talked a lot and I found out about my grandparents whom I had never known. And the mother I had never known either: a fun-loving teenager who was daft about dancing and whose favours had been much sought after by young men of her day. I learned how my serious, no-fun father had waited ten years for her to agree to marry him.

We strolled down the hill to my great-grandparents' house, standing still in its original state. It was a small whitewashed cottage with a thatched roof, tiny windows and rough, smoked-darkened walls.. A wooden platform, accessible by a ladder, ran round the area under the roof. The children had slept up there while the parents slept in the only bedroom downstairs. A chain hung down the chimney into the fireplace and here a black kettle sang gently all day, its contents always smelling of turf-smoke. There was a half-door which allowed light and air in during the day and over which the family donkey was wont to put his head in search of a tit-bit. Round the cottage were a few small fields where hay was grown to feed the animals and potatoes were grown to feed the humans. A peaty stream tripped happily along by the door, host to eels and brown trout. A heron was visiting it that summer that my aunt and I were there. For there were no humans to scare it away. My great-uncle, the youngest of thirteen children, had just died the previous year, aged ninety-eight and the house was now empty for the first time in over a hundred and fifty years. I stood by the ageless stream and thought of the sound of thirteen children running barefoot through the small fields and playing amongst the apple trees at the back of the house: children now long gone to dust, and I had a deep sense of how short our stay is on the earth, a butterfly span of time and space in the vastness of eternity. But my aunt stopped such morose thoughts with her anecdotes of life when she and my mother were young and used to spend summers in that very spot with their grandparents. She and mother were a wild pair by all accounts, dressing to kill, dancing till daylight, daring to differ, disapproved of by the locals. I thought of mother as I knew her and was confounded.

After a couple of weeks I asked Aunt Roisin if I might invite Mary down from Derry. She was more than happy about this and so I wrote to Mary. We met her off the bus a few days later, a bus full of people from Derry coming to stay at Portsalon because the

Troubles in the city were making life so difficult. As the summer wore on more and more people arrived. Most of them were women with small children who were feeling the danger of increased terrorist activity. They just squeezed in wherever they could. Old derelict cottages were opened up again after years of decay and farmers were letting out fields as caravan parks. Many had only tents or the already overcrowded homes of relatives, but all enjoyed the sense of freedom which the city lacked. Mary's grandparents who lived in the Creggan area of Derry had been burnt out and they were now staying with her parents. She was glad to get away. And I was glad of her company. We cycled miles on borrowed bikes along the winding country roads between high scented hedges and swam in the clear cool waters of the Swilly. We went to local dances where everybody from the age of three to a hundred and three seemed to congregate and where the showbands still held sway despite the arrival of the Beatles and other pop idols in Britain and the rest of the world. To this day I love the big band sound. It's so versatile. They played Irish ballads for the grannies, jigs and reels for the lively and Buddy Holly and Elvis Presley for romantics. Mary and I danced and sang along to everything, including a strange local dance called "Shoe the Donkey".

These dances tended to finish about three o'clock in the morning and the village shops opened so that we could buy icecream and cigarettes. This early hour of the morning was probably the busiest time of the day. Teenagers would hang around trying to get a date with someone they fancied or to cadge a lift home. When we finally got back to Portsalon, Mary and I used sometimes to swim at daybreak off Warden sands. This is one of the most relaxing experiences I have ever known; the soft hush of the waves whispering to the air, the touch of smooth sand underfoot, the buoyant water lifting and releasing me on the swell while all along the bay the early morning light picked out the luminous white border of the surf. My aunt thoroughly disapproved of our antics which made it all much more fun.

Despite the roughness of accommodation in the half-wrecked house and the need to find a place where the dock leaves grew greenest in order to answer a call of nature, those weeks in Donegal that summer of sixty-eight rank amongst my happiest ever. The sheer simplicity of life there was a tonic. I awoke every morning looking forward to the day: went to rest every night feeling fulfilled. It was with reluctance, therefore, that I packed my bags for home especially since I had half hoped to meet Pat again during my stay and I had seen no sign of him.

On my last Sunday morning I went to the remote little church at Massmount as usual and hung about outside in the windy churchyard which held the remains of so may of my ancestors, buried there beside Mulroy Bay, united by water with all those who had been forced into exile, three thousand miles away on the other side of the Atlantic. When as a child I had read The Forsaken Merman by Walter de la Mer, Massmount was the little church I imagined the children's mother to be praying in. Like them, the hope that a loved one might return kept me lingering till the last of the scattered worshippers slipped reverently inside.

People came to the chapel at Massmount from miles around on Sundays and holy days when its bell called them from far-flung cottages to fill its cold empty sanctuary with the warm breath of their prayers. When the second bell had rung and Mass was about to start I went in reluctantly because I knew there would be few seats left and I would need one, inclined as I was to faint when fasting for communion. Bitterly disappointed, I found it hard to concentrate on the liturgy, my thoughts alternating between memories of the terrible night of the fire and worry that he hadn't got away. As the ceremony proceeded I made the responses mechanically and after the Sanctus bells I lined up to go to the altar behind the other communicants. I had received the host and was making my way back to my seat when I saw him sign to me from the open door of the church so I continued down the aisle to the door, genuflected towards the altar and left.

Outside the church he took me in his arms and kissed me. His tongue found the sacred host in my mouth and slid it into his. Then he put his finger to his lips and gestured towards the hedge where I saw two bicycles half hidden in the leaves.

"I'm determined to have that cycle after all," he whispered and I blushed as I recollected the disastrous turn my life had taken after my refusal of his first offer.

"I wouldn't dare refuse again," I whispered back.

We headed off in silence towards Portsalon and made sure we were well out of earshot before we spoke aloud.

I know a wonderful place for a picnic breakfast," he said, "and I've got all the goodies stashed away in my saddle bag."

I smiled knowingly because I knew a wonderful place too and wondered if it was the same one. We whizzed down the last stretch of road to Portsalon crossroads, freewheeling, hands off the handlebars, enjoying the excitement in the sweet morning air. At the crossroads we turned left and began to pedal uphill. The warm breeze was so full of the heavy scent of meadow sweet that we felt almost drugged as we took in great lungfuls of air in our struggle towards Carablah and its secret lake. As I had guessed, his "perfect place" was the same as mine. We turned right across a little bridge just before my aunt's holiday house. Seeing it, I was about to speak, but he said, "I promise to talk about that later."

We found the hidden lake tucked serenely in its fold of hills and dismounted. Pat took out a rug and spread it on the ground and I flopped down exhausted. The peaty water glowed like dark topaz and the garland of white water lilies drifting on its surface shone with a soft luminous quality amidst the reflections of the surrounding hills. We were so completely alone we could've been Adam and Eve. Pat brought out a flask of tea and thick, buttered slices of fresh soda bread, chunks of local cheese and some fruit. I ate ravenously and thought about nothing except how good the food tasted and how perfect the lake was. Pat was silent and watchful while I ate. When I had finished he took both my hands in his and started to speak earnestly.

"Grainne, I had to see you at least this once. You have probably already worked out that I'm lying low. Please don't ask me questions that I can't answer. It's best you know nothing of what I'm doing. I only want you to understand that I believe what I'm doing is for the good of Ireland."

I shrugged my shoulders irritably. Pat tossed a small piece of white quartz into the water. It was only a tiny stone but the ripples from it spread out and out and out in ever-widening rings until they touched every edge of the lake.

"Our actions are like that," he said. "Once we make the first move they can spiral out of our control. I would never have hurt your aunt. I want you to know that."

"She'll soon be safely back in Scotland, so it doesn't matter," I said. "Let's just enjoy this day together."

"You're angry," he said. "Forgive me."

"For what?"

"For everything … your Uncle John, your aunt, dragging you here, messing up what we might've had together."

"Don't."

I pressed my hands to his lips because seeing him so miserable was unbearable. He clutched my hands in both of his and covered them with kisses. Then he took me into his arms and the sky enfolded us and we became as elemental as the water and the earth and the air around us. We touched each other here and there, reading each other's bodies like Braille. My breasts rose like the mountains round us and my thighs parted like the oceans below. The little freckles on my secret skin wheeled like constellations under his palm, my Lazarus body burning with resurrection. Ascension into heaven.

"Are you sure this is alright?" He whispered as I offered my body in complete surrender. I nodded. How could I deny such a man when his touch burned as brightly on me as Adam's first knowing kiss on Eve?

Afterwords we lay still together and drifted in and out of sleep through the long afternoon

"Take me to you, imprison me, for I,
   Except you enthral me, never shall be free
Nor ever chaste unless you ravish me."

Now I understood those lines from Donne's Holy Sonnet.

Towards evening the lengthening shadows of the hills fell across us and a chill stir of air told us it was time to go.

This time the freewheeling downhill was so very different. We were physically contented and our minds allowed a quiet space. We were borne along effortlessly like kites in a stiff breeze. The familiar landscape seemed newly created and bright. We cycled to the crossroads where Pat was to leave me

116

and just before we came into the village we stopped. Pat threw the bikes in the hedge and took me in his arms one last time.

"You'll have to go it alone from here," he said. "Leave the bike at the old house in Corry; I'll pick it up later. I don't want you to be associated with me. I love you too much for that."

"Can't I write or something?"

"Best not. It could put you in danger"
I thought, this day we've had together must be one of the best in the history of the world, and yet I might never see him again.

I shivered and, mistaking this for cold, he took a thick sweater out of his saddlebag and wrapped it round me, tying the sleeves around my neck. I snuggled into it all the way home. It smelt of wilderness and Pat When I got back to my aunt's house I had to struggle with a great reluctance to go in. Pat's touch still burned on me and it seemed as if I was still in a dream world and didn't want to wake up. There was a car outside which I didn't recognise and small talk with strangers was the last thing I felt capable of..

"You're very quiet, Grainne," Mary said, as I entered silently and sought out a seat in a dark corner of the room. "Had a good day?"

"Leave her," Mick said softly, "Can't you see she's exhausted? An early night for you, my girl," he said to me and I could tell by his eyes that he knew or suspected much of what had happened that day. He had come to pick up Mary. And me too if I was ready to leave.

Next day he drove me to the ferry. I was silent all the way, thinking of Pat.

"Want to talk about it?" he asked. I shook my head. He took a slip of paper from his pocket with a phone number on it. "My confidential help line. It's a charity I work for," he said. "Use it any time you need it, even in the middle of the night."

CHAPTER 11
"'tis you,'tis you must go and I must bide

As soon as I came to the border the hassle began. An officious prig of a customs officer ordered everybody off the bus and made us all open our cases. I think he must've had a knicker fetish because he insisted on taking out every pair of knickers in my case, even the soiled ones, and inspecting them, exactly what for, except to humiliate me, I have never learned. As I got to the outskirts of Derry there seemed to be a lot of RUC men around and the traffic flow was being very strictly controlled. When I finally arrived at Belfast Harbour there was a massive police presence and we all had to be searched again before we were allowed on the ferry. This was the first time that I saw how the Troubles affected the routine of ordinary life and had a taste of how difficult they might be to live with from day to day. We were only a couple of hours drive over the border but it was a different world.

Life at home was even more different. I had forgotten my father's bullying and my mother's stress. The family was still caught in its time-warp of bickering and Molly was still martyring herself on everybody's behalf. Mick had been called home when his grandparents were burned out and wouldn't be returning till the start of the university term. Thankfully that was drawing near.
But at least my absence seemed to have made my mother's heart grow fonder, though, and she was really pleased to see me home earlier than expected. I suppose she was actually worrying about losing Molly. And, of course, she had my father to deal with still. As soon as I arrived I could sense that he was all set to put me in Molly's place Fetching and carrying I could've put up with, but I was scared that it would

lead to other things and I was having none of it. Relations between us became strained very quickly because I was so much on my guard that I was barely civil to him. I was scared of what I might do to him if he laid a finger on me. Since my lovemaking with Pat I found it difficult to let anyone touch me even in an innocent way because I was trying to hold on to the memory of the special feel of his skin against mine. I used to sit up really late waiting for father to fall asleep before I went to my room. He would order me to go to bed but I would refuse and then he would lose his temper shouting that he would "swing for me" because I was so maddening and that one day I would push him too far and he would murder me. His shouting didn't bother me and I secretly thought that he might come off worst in a tussle with me now. It was just the thought of him prowling in the night that worried me. I started taking the poker to bed.

In the second week after I returned home Morag phoned to ask me to go "tattie howking" with her. The wages weren't bad and she, Emma and I would stay in a bothy together and it gave me an excuse to get away from my father. It would also stop me watching for the post every morning in the forlorn hope of a letter from Pat despite what he said about not involving me. When I had offered him my address he had said no because he was worried that in some dire emergency he might turn up on my doorstep and although I kept protesting that that would be fine by me, he was adamant that it was not a good idea. For these reasons I accepted Morag's offer gladly and the very next morning saw me heading for the potato fields of East Lothian.

I set off full of the joys, thinking what larks we three girls would have in the bothy; we would dye our hair, our underwear and the whole town red! I reckoned all the bending and movement from side to side would give me a beautiful waistline, the hard work would help me lose weight and the fresh air would give me a beautiful complexion. I think I must have read an old recruitment poster for the Land Army!

I always say my real education took place that summer in the potato fields. The work was back-breaking and mindless; the hours long and tedious with no respite. Hour after hour we followed the tractor and picked flat out to clear our stent before the driver came round again. There was no time for chat. There was barely time to breathe. By the end of each day our backs seemed permanently bent and, I for one, felt I would never be able to walk straight again. My daft idea that living in a bothy would be fun soon faded as I lay on my lumpy, makeshift bed, aching and yearning for a bath. The lack of decent cooking facilities combined with sheer exhaustion, meant that we never ate properly, just stuffed ourselves with bread and jam and were always hungry. I felt queasy almost all the time and craved sweet juicy oranges which were not available. I had no energy at the end of the working day for anything and frequently fell into bed unwashed. Only the thought that it would be over in a few weeks and a fierce determination not to give in kept me going. The realisation that some people worked as hard as this all their lives was truly shocking.

What I didn't appreciate was how different the world must look to people who had to work like that all their lives. I just found their company intolerable because of the crudeness of their speech and behaviour towards us and, to a lesser extent, each other. We girls were a constant source of ridicule because we were seen as "posh." They would've joyfully watched us fall down in the mud and be run over by the tractor. I had always assumed that only religion and colour produced fanatical hate. I learned that summer that you can be hated by others for no reason that makes sense to you at all. There is sometimes such a gulf between the way you see yourself and the way others see you that it's not possible to navigate to common ground. We were young and vulnerable. Like the other pickers, we were hard up, and prepared to work at a miserable job to earn our crust. The great divider was perhaps that we would not always be thus.

On one occasion when we were allowed to stop because the driving rain had turned the field into a quagmire my hands were stiff with cold and I dropped my flask of hot tea, dearer to me at that moment than any jewel. The spilt tea burnt my hand and I yelped in pain. But that was nothing to the pain inflicted by the yell of derisive laughter from the other pickers. This kind of thing was bad enough, but it was their disgusting remarks and gestures which caused me the most trouble. Grabbing body parts and referring to them and their functions by crude names was common. One of them asked me for a "man-hole cover" and shrieked with delight when it was obvious I had no idea what she meant. The others joined in the fun.

"Bloody big man-hole cover she needs."

"How do you ken?"

"Ah ken, that's all you need to ken."

"Go on, tell us."

"Because she's got a bloody big man-hole, that's why. Ah tried to have it off wi' her and it was like chucking a banana up the Clyde tunnel!"

Exchanges like these filled my dreams with disturbing scenarios that I couldn't shake off. I couldn't understand how something as beautiful and intimate as lovemaking could be spoken of in such ugly terms and in such a public way. The world never looked the same to me again.

Back in our student flat at the beginning of October, the "tattie-howking" weeks seemed to belong to a different world that we had somehow stumbled into by accident and had luckily managed to escape. I gave little thought to what mindless jobs the other pickers would be doing now that all the potatoes had been gathered in. Emma, Morag and I threw ourselves into university life with gusto, all of us aware, probably for the first time, of how lucky we were. We went to lectures and parties in about equal measure, lounged in cafes and gardens and then crammed till closing time in the libraries and reading rooms. We shopped till we dropped when we got our grants and then lived on beans and chips for weeks when the money ran low. And, of course, we had the chance to mix with students from all parts of the globe and gain a sense of the brotherhood of man.

We even took part in student demonstrations against things like raising overseas students' fees and having tutorials in our Wednesday afternoon free time. Demonstrations were always great fun. Usually we strolled down Princes Street with colourful banners and engaged in banter with shoppers. Then we would all crowd onto the steps of the National Gallery and make speeches which amused the crowd and gave foreign tourists a chance to practise their English by asking us questions. It was a wonderful existence and one I still feel privileged to have known.

But however hard I tried to throw myself into university life, I thought about Pat continually. Every morning I awoke to the sorrow of his absence and clung to my bed a little longer trying to capture the feeling of his long slow embrace. When I felt particularly low I would put on his jumper as reverently as the priest puts on his stole before saying Mass and I would allow myself the luxury of daydreaming. He and I would live in another world where there was no past and no hurt, only a golden future.

I felt sick nearly all the time and lost my vitality and my hair hung limply whatever I did with it. Morag and Emma noticed the change in me and were concerned. But I didn't feel I could tell even them about my yearnings for Pat and so I claimed that I just needed to get some healthy exercise. They persuaded me to go back to the university rowing club which I had been neglecting although I had enjoyed it so much in previous terms. They also decided that we would all go swimming together at least three times a week. It seemed to do the trick because I stopped feeling sick towards the end of term. I couldn't quite say when I started feeling better. I just realised one day that I did.

In rowing I found release from worry for a while. Trying to keep in perfect time with the others whilst listening to the cox kept my mind completely occupied as we skimmed down the Grand Union Canal, sometimes working the oars hard, sometimes resting them and enjoying the forward thrust our efforts had produced. It's a bit like freewheeling on a bike. For this reason I turned up for practice every Saturday morning no matter what the weather even though, as the winter set in, we sometimes had to break the ice on the canal surface to get the boat into the water.

On the last Saturday before the end of term we turned up at the boathouse as usual. There had been a hard frost over night and we were having difficulty breaking the ice. We eventually broke an area big enough to get the boat in the water, but we couldn't get it to push off because the ice around it would not give way. Those of us nearest the landing stage wedged our oars against it to get some purchase to push off. My oar slipped under the landing stage and dislodged rubbish that had gathered there. I pulled the boat closer to the plastic sack to take it on board because we tried to keep the area round the boathouse clean despite the fact that many people used the canal as a dumping ground.

It was a clear plastic bag and as I took it in my hand my heart stopped. I screamed and dropped it back into the water. The others quickly pulled the boat over and recovered the bag from the water. Jenny, the cox, vomited, Karen screamed. Not wishing to look on the horror again, I volunteered to go for the police. When I got back the rest of the crew were huddled in the boathouse and the bag was lying on the bank covered with a jacket. The police came and moved it into their van before they started questioning us. They also needed the names and addresses of all other members of the rowing club and questioned us so closely that we each felt under suspicion of the terrible crime.

It was a baby's face, blue with cold, eyes popping with suffocation, that had stared at me from the bag. Sweet Jesus, I thought, what could drive anybody to do a thing like that?

The police established that the baby had been only hours old and still alive when it was put in the bag. They broadcast an appeal for the mother to come forward for medical treatment, but no one ever did. It's hardly surprising. A woman so desperate to conceal a pregnancy that she disposed of her baby in that barbaric way was hardly in a state to be concerned about her own health. Or so I reasoned. I could imagine some unfortunate young woman, weakened by labour and terror struggling down the mucky canal bank in the dead of night to stuff her murdered baby under the landing stage. But I could not begin to imagine any circumstance that would drive her to do such a thing. Deeply perturbed. I lay in bed wondering if her parents were even more rooted in Victorian morality than my own. Would they have locked her up at home or put her in an institution? Or would they just have made her burn with shame for the rest of her life as mine would have done? And what of the baby's father? Where was he in her hour of need? Whatever the circumstances she had obviously been driven to the edge.

We all felt sullied as if in some way we were touched with the crime of the poor woman who had borne and destroyed her own baby in secrecy and shame. The carefree student days eating Knickerbocker glories at the Chocolate House and wandering through the cobbled streets of the Grassmarket looking for joss sticks and big earrings were tinged with guilt now and we were all glad, I think, to break up for the Christmas holidays.

CHAPTER 12

"But come ye back when summer's in the meadow

Christmas at home was a melancholy affair that year.
We missed Molly who had gone to spend the festive
period with Mick's parents and my father's outbursts
of uncontrollable temper were proving almost
impossible to live with. Because all his arteries were
hardened an operation was out of the question and the
doctor had prescribed warfarin which is rat poison
and, I thought, entirely appropriate for someone like
him. The meal on Christmas Day was a nightmare.
His high blood pressure meant he was not allowed salt
and nothing tasted right to him without it. All the way
through dinner he slated my mother's cooking skills,
pushed plates of food aside and ranted about what a
useless family he had and how a man scourged with a
life amongst seven women might at least have had
one who could cook.

"I wouldn't be surprised if you're trying to
poison me with this muck," he said. "After all you'll
be a rich widow when I die. To think I've worked
hard and paid my dues all my life to leave you in
luxury to squander my money."
Unfortunately he was forbidden alcohol so we
couldn't even mellow things with a nice bottle of
wine or a couple of sherries. He had also been advised
to stop smoking but he was too severely addicted to
even attempt giving up and smoked one cigarette after
another at the table so that our food, our clothes and
our hair were enveloped in a fug of tobacco. I wanted
to shout or even slap him but remained civil because
of the others. My mother tried hard to appease him
when he didn't want to be appeased. But my younger
sister Kate impressed me by being able to behave as if
he didn't exist! She ate her food with relish, answered

him in monosyllables if he addressed her directly and completely ignored his bad temper. He just wanted to throw tantrums and give us a bad time. If mum and I had been able to behave as she did he would have been at a loss for someone to torment. But he never failed to get through our armour with some barb or other and was particularly cruel to my mother.

"The worms in Strabane Cemetery will be having a rotten Christmas dinner too. Your old mother can't be too tasty," was the comment that finally got the tears flowing.

When I could escape I would walk for miles. There was a lovely country road that led away from the dockyard area of Rosyth in which we lived to the picturesque little coastal village of Limekilns. I would amble along taking in the freshness of the air no matter what the weather trying to rest my brain from the atmosphere in the house. The tiny cemetery drew me to sit amongst the gravestones, take Uncle John's little pipe out of my pocket and turn it over and over in my hands like a holy relic as I remembered him. It seemed so unfair to me that a good man like him should've endured so much and died so early when a man like my father was still around. I found that if I sat quite still and looked out to sea I could recapture every detail of that wonderful Christmas that I had shared with Uncle John and Pat. It was like turning over the pages of a fairytale. I remembered the tree hung with coloured glass balls and the glitter of rime and starlight on the holly boughs, thick with berries. I could smell cinnamon and warm Irish coffees as if they were wafting over the sea to me. I could taste the rain on Pat's glowing cheek when he stooped under the doorway and kissed me in the pool of soft yellow lamplight. When I could taste the salt tears on my own cheeks as I remembered my loss I would get up, stiff with cold, and walk slowly home.

We had no telephone and neither did my friends and so at home I was deprived of their friendly girlish chatter. Never before had I realised just how important it was to me. Sometimes I sat in my freezing cold room and poured my heart out to Emma in long letters. Sometimes I posted them, but often I did not because on re-reading I felt my thoughts were too dire to saddle anyone else with.

When my parents talked at all it was about the Troubles in Ireland with which they seemed to be obsessed. I hated this, having made every effort since my last encounter with Pat to shut out any news of them, uncomfortably aware of my dangerous secret. I would switch channels or leave the room if there was any mention of the civil unrest on television. But it cropped up everywhere. Newspapers, radios, even people in bus queues seemed to have nothing else to talk about. Things were getting so bad in Ireland that it became impossible to escape news of it and on the mainland so many fools had started making hoax bomb calls that they were becoming a regular occurrence in schools and shopping malls, constant reminders of the very real bombs placed in shops, cafes and supermarkets that were creating carnage in Ireland.

Even on a trip with mother to the January Sales in Edinburgh it became the focus of our day. We had just gone into Woolworths which was pretty crowded when a voice over the tannoy system said, "Ladies and gentlemen this is the manager speaking. Will customers please vacate the store immediately. Leave by the nearest exit. There is no need for panic."

Even before the announcement had finished words like "bomb" and "IRA" were being bandied about and people were stampeding for the main door. As they piled out into the street my mother said to me in this really loud voice, shouting over the traffic noise, "In

the name of God, did you ever hear anything so silly in your life? What would the IRA want to bomb Woolworths for, especially in Princes Street?"
To me she suddenly sounded so Irish that I was terrified for her.

"Let's move away from here," I said.

"What would be the point of blowing up Woolworth's in Princes Street?" She asked even louder.
People began to stare at her and particularly at the very large shopping bag she was carrying. I mean she could have hidden half a ton of gelignite in there. She was oblivious to them. .

"They're eejits …" she began.

"Shut up," I hissed and, grabbing her by the arm, I propelled her through the crowds. She turned to me with a look of total surprise. Later when we were safely out of earshot I told her why I was anxious for her.

"I was scared they might turn on you and tear you apart. Have you any idea how people on the mainland feel about the IRA?"
She tried to be dismissive but I could see that she was shaken.

I began to curse the Troubles more and more because they interfered with my life. Despite my best efforts I still retained my Irish vowel sounds and people who met me for the first time often asked me where I came from. Because of my place of birth it was impossible for me to escape being tarred with the green or the orange brush. When people asked me where I came from I used to say Derry. This was the name given to my native city at home and school and is in fact an Anglicisation of the Irish name Doire meaning an oak grove, and the name given to the city in ancient times because it is said Saint Columba built it on the site of an oak grove. But I soon realised that if I called my native city Derry people assumed I was Catholic, Nationalist and an IRA sympathiser.

I then started referring to my birthplace as Londonderry as this was the title used by the media. But I found people then assumed that I was Protestant, Loyalist and a Paisleyite. There seemed to be no way I could just be Northern Irish. Nor could I just say I was Irish since none of the Southern accents sound at all like the North and at that time people South of the border referred to us as coming from "the black North".

Eventually I started saying I came from the Western Isles as that accent bears similarities to mine and not many people know what it sounds like anyway. I was young and healthy and just wanted to have fun and I considered the whole business of fighting over religion totally stupid.

I used to play John Lennon's "Imagine" all the time because I thought he definitely had the right idea and I felt very lucky to be living in a beautiful city like Edinburgh where people could get on with their lives unhampered by bigotry. I began, in fact, to scorn religion seeing only the difficulties it caused. After all many of my friends didn't go to church but their lives didn't seem any less happy or good. When, however, I tried skipping Mass some Sundays I felt guilty and I found the habit of prayer very difficult to break. All my life I had prayed for anything I needed, even things like good results in my exams and I felt free to party and stay up late safe in the knowledge that God was looking after me. I once spent the night on the beach at Gullane to watch the sunrise and got to my nine o'clock exam exhausted and half an hour late, but confident that God would see me through. When I passed I said a prayer of thanks-giving. I felt so lucky that I had a direct hot-line to the Almighty that I realised I would have to work at becoming a heathen.

By way of contrast, my family prayed constantly for an end to the Troubles, listening with bated breath to every news bulletin. They were always worried about friends and family back home. Sometimes mother would shed a tear over the news and say, "There'll be sore hearts in Derry tonight."

Streets she had roamed in all her days had been reduced to rubble and shops she had loved had been bombed out of existence.

But there was only one person I really feared for and I could not mention him to anybody. Every time I heard about a fatality in Northern Ireland my heart would stop till I heard the name. Despite all the evidence to the contrary, I insisted on believing that only people who somehow asked for it, actually got hurt. I suppose it's easier to think like that, because it absolves you from all responsibility to take action. It was only when the Troubles struck my own family that I was forced to face the bitter truth.

Meanwhile there were parties to be had and games to be played and the fullness of student life to be enjoyed. I had joined a mixed hockey team the winter of my first term, as the compulsory woman. We played on cinder pitches and we played rough. It was the nearest I could get to camogy. I met a bloke during these sporting activities who greatly took my fancy. He played hockey for the Catholic Students' Union and we went for a coffee or two at The Catacombs after matches.

When I returned to university for the spring term we started dating. I suppose I was trying to forget Pat, I don't know. Chris was good-looking in a homely kind of way, not given to expensive or showy clothes or indeed anything that might draw attention to himself. He was a caring sort of person and a good listener and sometimes quite amusing too, with his ability to make faces and put on funny voices. Looking back, he probably reminded me of Pat. Something, anyway, gave me the hots for him. We went out for a couple of months and he never once tried it on, so I reckoned he respected me and I took him home for mother's approval. And I think she did approve although she didn't actually say so. She simply refrained from finding fault with him. We had a whirlwind romance and Chris asked me to get engaged. I agreed because I liked the idea of a beautiful ring and I thought our relationship might progress beyond a goodnight kiss on the doorstep. Marriage never entered my head.

We had a party and I got the ring on my twenty-first birthday in March. I had invited all the family but only the twins and their husbands came. No doubt they saw it as a chance to get back into the family fold, but, sadly, most of my family did not feel at ease in a student environment.

Morag nudged me during the evening and said, "You know what they say: when you get the ring, you get the thing."

I wasn't so sure, but I hoped I might get more than his customary peck on the cheek. When nearly everyone had gone and Chris started to clear up I called him over and drew him down on the sofa beside me. I kissed him long and passionately till I heard his breathing grow deep and slow. Then I ran my hands over his chest and felt his tiny nipples grow erect. I moved my lips to his neck and started caressing his throat, gradually nibbling my way round to the really sensitive area at the top of the collarbone. I took his earlobes in my mouth and sucked them. I could feel his penis stirring and then harden. I gently moved a hand to his inner thigh and stroked him there. He began to moan with desire so I moved my hand to his zip, opened it slowly and put my hand inside his trousers. He was wonderfully hard. My own breathing was just beginning to get out of control when he jumped up and said,

"We shouldn't be doing this."

"Why not?" I said, a bit miffed that he'd ruined the moment.

"You're a decent Catholic girl and you ask me that!" he said, tidying his clothing.

"It's natural to explore each other," I said, rolling my eyes in disbelief.

"If we can't wait we'll have to get married sooner," he said.

"Marriage!" I shouted. "I don't want to get married."

I wonder if I hold the record for the shortest engagement in history. Shame, the ring was so nice. At least I now understood Ian's situation when I had rebuffed him and was at last able to forgive him. But I felt a fool again. And as for men, I was as confused as ever. I decided it was probably best to stick to Shakespeare. At least he was safely dead. And the characters in his plays often had happy marriages, although they seemed for the most part to be so unaware of the shape of the human form that women constantly mistook other women for men and vice-versa. Since Shakespeare seemed to understand all other human emotions such as jealousy, ambition ingratitude and crippling indecisiveness, I had reason to hope that he might be right about love too. I decided to wait till love found me and hoped I would recognise my prince charming even if he were wearing a frock. And indeed, I did go out with a man in a frock and got myself in another fine mess.

It was just as well that my relationship with Chris ended abruptly. I shudder to think what might have become of us both if I had got more deeply involved with him, good-living boy that he was.

The morning after the party I felt pretty bad about letting him down and angry with myself for making such a fool of myself. I did not want company and my heart sank when Maryanne and Calum appeared in the kitchen. Everybody else had gone home.

"Can I have this last bag of cheese and onion crisps?" I asked, opening the bag and stuffing crisps in without waiting for an answer.

"You preggie or something?" Calum asked. "You certainly seem to have a craving for crisps." I was shocked. My face must have drained of colour.

"Calum!" Maryanne looked daggers at him.

"Just ignore him," she said.

"Sorry, just joking," he said.

But she gave me a searching look which I found very disturbing. And then a terrible thought crossed my mind. What if I was? I felt panic begin to overwhelm me and my head started to spin.

"You all right, Grainne?" Maryanne leaned over me. "Go and have a lie down. You didn't get much sleep last night."

I didn't know how I was going to get through the rest of the weekend with them. I was completely preoccupied by the terrible thought that I just might be pregnant. My periods had always been few and far between, coming roughly every four or five months, and so the absence of a period did not mean anything to me. Now I counted up and realised that I hadn't seen one for over six months. I had had the last one in Ireland. I remembered being amused after blowing the windows out of the house and thinking I wouldn't have done it if I hadn't been premenstrual.

Calum obviously felt the need to break the silence he had caused.

"You're well out of Ireland, Geraldine, you certainly made a good choice when you decided on Edinburgh. Queen's in Belfast is full of bloody troublemakers sticking their noses into politics when it's none of their business. That's the problem with educating the lower classes, they get too uppity, think they know everything, think they can set the world to rights overnight."

Maryanne nudged him but he ignored her.

"Do you know that lot marched from Belfast to Londonderry to make trouble?"

"I thought their protest was about civil rights," I said, unwillingly drawn in. "And wasn't it meant to be peaceful?"

" Civil rights! They're lucky they've got a vote at all! Somebody should've dumped the lot of them over the bridge at Burntollet"

"You know I don't like you talking politics." Maryanne said. "Anyway students always get involved in protests. It's part of the course."

"So true," I said in a jocular tone, just wanting to get him off the Northern Ireland thing. "Even I got involved in the protest against the rise in overseas students fees ... walked down Princess Street waving a placard ..."

"Overseas students? Let them pay is what I say!" He looked ready for an argument but I felt the panic attack was still coming on and rushed from the kitchen.

As soon as I could gain the privacy of my own room I examined my body. Had it changed? There was definitely a small mound below my waistline, but then, we'd all put on weight because of our stodgy diet when potato picking. On and off, I had felt flutters in my stomach which I had taken to be butterflies because I was pretty stressed out a lot of the time. Now I was thinking could it be I felt a baby stirring? I felt the panic rise again. The floor was coming up to meet me and stars were floating round my head. God, no. I couldn't even think about that. I was glad to see Maryanne and Calum off because now that it was obvious to me that I was pregnant I was sure it was obvious to everyone else as well. As soon as they were safely on the train, I headed for the medical library and took out books on pregnancy and childbirth. I stuffed them guiltily in my bag as if they were pornography and hurried back to the flat and locked the door before I dared take them out. I stared at the drawings of wombs with babies in them and tried to relate them to me. It couldn't be. I couldn't imagine it. But then I read the text about body changes during pregnancy and I looked at my dark nipples and the small swelling round my middle and I knew that I was definitely at least six months gone. My first reaction was shame. I had been brought up to believe that this was about the worst thing a girl could do. Saint Maria Gorretti and others like her had died willingly rather than do such a thing. I didn't think about how I was going to cope or how I was going to tell people. I just felt deep burning shame that I had let my mother down and a certainty that, what ever else came to pass, I would make sure she never found out.

CHAPTER 13

"Or when the valley's white and hushed with snow"

I wrote home telling my mother that I wouldn't be seeing them all for a while because of my studies. Now that I was in my second year, I explained, I had to study much harder. There was a certain amount of truth in this and I had no idea how I was going to manage. But other matters were more urgent and I would deal with them first. Next I went out and bought myself more smocks, which, fortunately were really in fashion and would arouse no suspicion whatsoever. I was really grateful for even this small mercy. I decided I would definitely tell nobody, not even Emma and Morag. I had worked out that the baby, which could only be Pat's, was due around the middle of April. Hopefully it would arrive during the Easter vacation when my flatmates would be away. I didn't think what would happen after that. I didn't allow myself to. I just kept breathing in and hoped to hide my terrible secret.

The Easter holidays came and my friends departed in early April. They were surprised to learn that I wasn't going home, but accepted the explanation I had already given my mother. They had both opted to do ordinary degrees and finish at the end of third year whereas I would have to get merits in my second year subjects if I wanted to do Honours.

They were hardly out the door before I locked it and started doing breathing exercises as instructed by my books. I also assembled the few things that I thought I would need, like clean towels, extra sheets, a basin and sponge and a blanket to wrap the baby in as well as scissors and string as instructed by the midwifery book, but I was not too sure I would be able to use them. It all seemed quite straightforward to me.

Which just goes to show that ignorance is bliss. If I had had any idea of the terrifying time ahead of me I would probably have thrown myself off the Forth Bridge rather than face it. But because I knew no better, I was not all that worried about the actual birth. Reckoning that I had about two weeks to go, I stocked up on food and magazines and decided to loaf about the flat. But very quickly, I found this plan impossible, because it gave me too much time to think. So I began a programme of cleaning the flat from top to bottom, intending to scrub the skirting boards, shampoo the carpets and turn the mattresses as well as the daily jobs, allowing myself to stop only for meals. I'd done the carpets and skirting boards before I got completely sick of the whole business and felt I just had to get out. The bright April sun had wakened me earlier than usual and I was restless. I knew Princess Street Gardens would be full of flowers and birds and I could stay indoors no longer so I packed a picnic and took the bus up Leith walk. The spring sunshine lit up thousands of daffodils running down the slope from the castle and all over the grass bright little crocus flowers cheered in splashes and pools of purple and white and yellow. The first delicate leaves were appearing on the trees and I was poignantly aware, as I had been once before, of rebirth all around me and my own life desolate and destroyed. I put my cold hands in my pocket and found Uncle John's pipe there and thought of him dead and gone forever and yearned for the days we had known. He was the only person I could possibly have confided my present condition to. And he would have known what to do. In a different time I might have been overjoyed at the imminent arrival of Pat's baby and I would surely have hoped for a son so that I could call him John. Now I was lonely and scared and desperate, overwhelmed by the total mess that was my life.

"You all right love?" A kind passer-by spoke to me and broke into my thoughts. I realised I was crying and felt really embarrassed.

"Yes, fine thanks," I said and bolted towards the shops to lose myself in anonymity.

Heedless, I ran straight into a baby shop and straight out again. There was no way that I was buying a single baby item. It would just make things harder when the time came. Instead I went into C&A and buzzed up and down the escalators pretending to be looking for something. Suddenly something warm trickled down my legs and at the same time my face burned scarlet. Realising my waters had broken, soaking my underwear and seeping into the electrics of the escalator, I waddled as fast as I could out of the shop. If only Emma and Morag had been there we could've had a good laugh about it. Alone, I was terrified, expecting the baby to arrive at any minute so I got a taxi back to the flat.

As soon as I got indoors I started preparations, filled a bowl with cool water to set by my bed for mopping my hot face and a bottle of drinking water for the thirsty work ahead. I changed the covers on the bed and piled up fresh towels on the floor next to it. Then I got into a big loose nightie. But nothing more seemed to be happening and I curled up, relieved, on the settee with one of my library books to read and see if this was normal. About midnight I decided to have a nice hot bath and go to bed.

It was probably the bath that did it. Suddenly the most incredible pain shot through my lower body like some invisible force was tearing me in two. I cried out involuntarily. Jesus, I thought, if this is just the first pain what will the last one be like? I tried to climb out of the bath and another pain seized me making it impossible to move. I waited, one foot on the floor, one in the bath until it passed. Then I got my back to the wall and inched along it into the bedroom, grabbing a towel as I went. I sat on the bed and timed my contractions as the books had told me. They were coming every three minutes so I realised I had gone straight into heavy labour and the baby would arrive in a few hours. But even one hour seemed an impossible length of time to endure pain like this. I lay on the bed and tried to remember how to do my breathing exercises. They helped a bit but the pain was still unbearable and I had to pace the floor, bracing myself against the wall or a chair each time a contraction came, crying out to God, asking what I had done to deserve such misery and, eventually, exhausted, I lay on the floor whimpering. I felt like a helpless ewe struggling to lamb and would've died gladly there and then. I remembered as a child in Ireland watching fascinated as a dead cow with a calf's head sticking out of it's rear end was hoisted onto the knacker's lorry. I thought, they will find me lying like that when they come back after the. holidays. And I didn't care.

Then I thought of Uncle John and what he had suffered and I was ashamed of my weakness. And just as I determined to be braver the most violent need to push seized me and I felt my whole insides were being forced out of my body. It was terrifying. None of the books warned me of this level of pain and so I thought there must be something badly wrong and I would indeed die there alone. Another pushing pain gripped me, and another. I managed to stagger to my feet. All my instincts told me to bear down with this pain. I went into the hallway and grasped the newel post of the stair and squatted. I pushed and pushed and pushed with the pain again and again and again. I felt the baby's head against the small opening of my vagina and thought, oh God, no, just as the biggest contraction of all caused me to issue a blood-curdling scream which I couldn't believe was mine. The baby's head appeared between my legs. The next push produced the rest of my daughter.

I hunkered along, half crawling, with her still attached to me, through the living area and into the bedroom where I had left the scissors and string to deal with the umbilical cord. I fumbled and struggled to do as the book had instructed and was able to lift the baby clear of the horrible grey sinewy tube and lay her on the bed before the next pain came and brought the afterbirth. I was disgusted by the big bloody jellyfish blob that came out of me, not expecting it to be so large and loathsome. I struggled out of my nightie, rolled the revolting thing up in it and put it aside.

Then I picked up the baby and struggled into bed with her against my breast and dropped immediately into an exhausted sleep.

Much, much later I awoke. At first I was struggling through a fog of sleep and exhaustion and thought I was wakening out of a nightmare. When I became fully conscious I realised I was living, not dreaming, this nightmare. Every bit of me ached, but especially the tender place through which the baby had torn her way into my world. I was scared to look at her, half of me hoping for a stillbirth and the other half ashamed of the thought. I had to force myself to look at her properly for the first time. Her dark curls were matted and stuck to her head with dried mucus and blood. Her eyes were puffy and closed tight in her face swollen and the snag of umbilical cord was disgusting. But she was alive and sleeping peacefully. The most beautiful little thing I had ever seen. I was overcome with a ludicrous sense of pride! This was definitely the greatest achievement of my life to date. I cradled her to me, at a loss how to deal with my unexpected and completely overwhelming feeling of maternal love. This was going to make doing what I had to do so much harder.

For hours I lay wondering what to do next, too scared to get out of bed because I didn't think my legs would hold me. Eventually I had to try to get up because I had finished the jug of water beside the bed and I was hungry and thirsty. I used the sponge from the basin prepared hours earlier to give my face a wash. This refreshed me enough to make me get out of bed. I could hardly walk, but somehow I managed to get to the kitchen and butter bread and make a pot of tea which I wolfed greedily. Then I had a bath.

All the time the baby slept. After my bath I laid her on a towel and sponged her gently with warm water. She started to cry and my breasts began to drip so I wrapped her up in a towel and put her on to suckle. Quite soon we were both asleep again. And so our first day together was done.

Next time we woke the bed was in a mess and I had to struggle out and change it. I cut up some of the towels I had laid out and used them as nappies. I found myself chatting to her as I did this and knew that she would have to go soon before I got too attached. I wondered how far I could walk because I didn't want to risk getting a bus in case someone might remember me later.

She was only four days old and I was still pretty groggy when I wrapped her up carefully in a warm blanket, pulled an old woolly hat of mine on her head, put her into my sports bag and zipped it. To my everlasting shame, I had decided to leave her on a doorstep in one of the posh areas of town.

My first thought was to leave her in Royal Terrace, a beautiful street full of big Victorian houses and up-market hotels, looking out on Calton Hill. But it was too near my flat and I thought if there was a search, the area around where they found her would be the most likely place to start. I trudged on up Leith Walk but by the time I reached Princess Street I knew I had to get a bus. I finally decided on Newington which was a mixture of expensive houses, small hotels and Residential Homes for the elderly. The first place I picked out was an old folks' home. I reckoned it would have trained carers and loads of incontinence pads and I knew grannies love babies. I thought it would be ideal. So, without opening the bag to look at her in case I chickened out, I popped the bag under a tree at the entrance and retired across the road to wait and make sure she got picked up. I hung about for ages until my feet were numb and my backed ached with the cold. But nobody came in or went out of the building. House of the living dead, I thought and a shiver ran down my spine. I had read Roald Dahl's Landlady. She had stuffed the bright parrot in its pretty gilded cage, she had stuffed the cosy cat that curled up on the mat before the blazing fire and she had stuffed her handsome young lodgers.

I ran across the road and grabbed the bag. It was ominously quiet and still. My heart started to race. What if she'd died of cold? I put the bag on the pavement and squatted down beside it, pretending to rummage in it. Her hands were frozen. I started to chafe them frantically. She didn't stir. Jesus, I though, Sweet Jesus, she's dead. I grabbed her out of the bag and shook her roughly. She cried and I was so relieved I wept, rocking backwards and forwards on my heels, cuddling her, saying, "I'm sorry, I'm sorry," over and over again.

A few people were staring at me so I grabbed the bag and hurried away with her still in my arms to the nearest bus stop.

"You're a horror, that's what you are. Thought you'd give me a fright, didn't you wee smelly?" I said to her teasingly as I put her back in the bag.

I got on the first bus that came along. It was going down the Bridges so I went that way. As we drove over the South Bridge and I looked down on Waverley Station below I thought what an ideal place it would be to leave a baby in the hope that she would be spotted and taken care of. I wandered into the station, left the big red sports bag sitting conspicuously in the reception area and sat some distance away to see what would happen. I noticed soon that people were giving the bag a very wide berth and casting anxious glances at it. After about fifteen minutes a British Rail official arrived, brought by a member of the public. I was aghast at the conversation that ensued!

"I'll cordon the area off," the official was saying, "Call in the bomb disposal people."
I shot from my hiding place and grabbed the bag with a muttered apology. I climbed into the first taxi I could find and went home.

"You win, buggerlugs," I said to her as I took her out of the bag once more. "I suppose I'd better feed you."
I slumped into a chair with relief, leaving the problem for tomorrow.

That night I slept little, drifting in and out of terror. Sometimes the baby was stuffed and displayed in the crib in a nativity scene, sometimes she was blown up in the sports bag, sometimes she was stuck inside me and couldn't come out and I was doomed to push forever and ever till I died. Several times I awoke soaking with sweat and breathing hard. But somehow the nightmares told me what I must do next.

Next morning I looked out the phone number Mick had given me and dialled it. Even before he answered it I could feel relief wash over me. I knew he would not let me down. While it was ringing and ringing I was rehearsing what I would say. How much did he need to know?

"Good morning, Mick here."
He sounded so far away that I burst into tears.
"Take your time," he said gently, "Sure there's no hurry at all."

"It's me, Geraldine, Grainne," I managed at last.

"What's wrong love? You sound desperate." I poured out my whole sorry tale in a muddled incoherent confession, even the shameful bit about trying to abandon the poor wee baby.

"Go and make yourself a nice cup of tea," he said, "I'll be with you as soon as I can, I promise."

"But what about your work?"

"Today you are my work. I'll see you as soon as I can. God bless."

"Don't bring Molly. Don't tell her … or anyone."

"I wasn't going to. Molly knows my work is confidential. She respects that. Now, I'll have to get a move on to have any hope of seeing you today."

Why, oh why, hadn't I thought of him sooner? My heart felt lighter for the first time since Calum had posed that awful question, "You preggie or something?" I picked up the baby and danced around singing a daft song my mother used to sing to us:

"Shake hands with your uncle Mick, my dear
And here's your sister Kate
And here's the girl you used to kiss
Down by the garden gate."

Then I started tidying the flat and looking in cupboards to see what I had to offer him to eat. Unable to settle to anything till he arrived, I didn't even think about eating myself.

Mick arrived around teatime, laden with bags of shopping. He had obviously spent some time in Princess Street on the way down. I threw my arms around him and did not want to stop hugging him in case it was all just a daft dream and I would wake up. The bags were mainly from Marks and Spencers and I was desperate to wade in amongst them, but Mick made me sit down. He had a good look at me and then the baby before he said, "Eat first, then surprises," as

146

if I was just a child. From one of the bags he produced a delicious ready meal and a bottle of wine. I insisted on laying the table. I would've liked to put candles on it but I was scared he might think me silly. But before we sat down he himself produced a candle and flowers from a bag and placed them on the table. "In honour of my new niece," he said. How was I going to tell him that I did not intend to keep her?

After the meal he cleared the dishes away while I was allowed to look in the bags full of lovely baby things, pretty dresses and gowns as well as practical items like nappies. I was dying to try them on her, but she was a bit grubby and I was scared to bath her because she was so tiny. He saw me trying to sponge her down on a towel and suggested we give her a proper bath in a basin. It was awkward but between us we managed. His suit trousers got covered in baby powder and fluff from the towels into the bargain but he didn't seem to mind.

"I need the practice. I hope it'll be Molly's turn soon. We want to start a family as soon as we're married," he said, "and I'll be a dab hand at this and she'll think she's got a great catch."

I laughed and danced around with the baby, putting off the serious talk as long as possible.

"Let's get the wee one down for the night and sit and watch TV like an old married couple," said Mick, laughing. He took her from my arms with a gentleness that was touching to see. "Where does she sleep?"

"In bed with me."

"Are you sure that's a good idea? I mean you'll not get much rest with a baby beside you."

"There's no where else."

He took her through to the bedroom I had indicated and came back after ten minutes grinning from ear to ear.

"I've just found the baby a cot," he said.

I went into the room and froze in horror. The baby was lying in a coffin. An involuntary cry broke from my lips.

"What is it? What is it, Grainne? You look like you've seen a ghost."

I pointed to the brown box, but at that moment I recognised it as the drawer from the old dressing table in Emma's room, the room I had allocated Mick. He had made up a little bed for the baby in the drawer. Red with embarrassment and full of apologies he said,

"I only thought to make her safe. Forgive me for being an interfering fool."

"It's not your fault. I've had such dreams. I think I'm going off my head."

"Tonight you will sleep. I am here to take care of you both. I'll take her into bed with me if you like and wake you if she needs you."

I knew she was better off in the makeshift cot and agreed to leave her there. After all it would be best to get used to being without her. Mick ran me a bath and made me a cup of milky cocoa and I eventually slept very contentedly that night knowing he was around. Next morning he insisted on taking us both to be checked by a doctor despite my loud and sustained protests. I was still finding it hard to admit that I had had a baby at all. But he was not to be put off and we were both duly checked and found healthy. Next he took me to register the baby, an act I found even harder because I was forced to give her a name, to my mind, an even greater recognition of her existence. I called her Patricia after her father because I couldn't give her his surname. Afterwards Mick insisted on a little celebration by having lunch out. He bought a kind of sling that supported the baby as I carried her against my chest, freeing my hands. People looked at us admiringly as if we were a lucky young couple out showing off our new baby. I was dreading the moment when he would say he had to go, but I knew it would be fairly soon.

When we got back to the flat Mick asked me if I had christened Patricia when she was born. He was just being polite. He knew the answer. I hadn't even thought about it which is a terrible indictment of a good Catholic girl. I was obviously forgetting my roots. He asked me if we could do it there and then and have a blessing in the church later. when the opportunity arose. I dressed her in the prettiest gown he had bought her and got dressed myself in the nicest clothes I could fit into. Mick suggested we use the washing up bowl as a makeshift baptismal font and pour the water over her head with a cream jug. I lived in a student flat. We used milk straight from the bottle. A cream jug was not to be found. In the end I held her over the sink and Mick ran a trickle of water from the tap over her forehead, saying, "I baptise thee, Patricia, in the name of the Father and of the Son and of the Holy Ghost, Amen."

That night while Patricia slept we had the serious talk I had been dreading. Mick accepted at last that I could not keep the baby. He thought adoption might be too final and anyway there was no way I could face the sheer bureaucracy involved at that time He suggested fostering, but it seemed too impermanent to me and I felt at any moment she might come bouncing back. Mick finally agreed to take her to Ireland and find some family member to look after her while I sorted myself out. He seemed to feel that once I was in a job I would want to make a home for her myself. I wasn't so sure, but didn't say so and made him swear to keep her parentage secret.

He stayed a few more days till we got Patricia used to bottle-feeding and then he set off to Ireland with her. Because we didn't have a carry-cot Mick reluctantly placed the baby in the sports bag I offered, accepting that she would be able to sleep better that way. It made it easier not to actually see the baby as he walked away and perhaps it was easier for him too. It's not every day a guy finds himself literally holding the baby. I cried, but, in truth, parting with him was the bigger wrench, parting with Patricia was a relief. Now I could get on with my life.

CHAPTER 14

"It's I'll be here in sunshine or in shadow"

"I go, I come back?"
"Emma!"
I got out of bed as fast as I could. It was nearly midday and Emma had returned from holiday, daft and loveable as ever. This was her favourite line from all the Peter Seller's films we watched. I was a bit emotional so she put on her silly accent and said it again. Soon I was hearing every detail of her adventures over the holidays, mainly involving the vet bloke and her mother who didn't seem to see eye to eye with him which didn't surprise me at all. This was the first time that she had taken him home to meet the family and her account was screamingly funny, punctuated as it was with dramatic actions. Her mother had brought out all the best dishes and produced a Sunday meal fit for royalty. The boyfriend had turned up with spatters of blood all over his glasses so that he could scarcely see through them and rings of blood round his wrists where he had washed only his hands and pulled his shirt down over his bloody arms. He had only just finished helping to de-horn cattle, he explained, and had been in a terrific hurry. He had got the measure of her mother pretty quickly, which wasn't surprising, Emma said, since her lips were puckered like a tight anus that wouldn't even let the world have it's excess wind! He then deliberately played the country bumpkin and ate his main course with his pudding spoon and his ice cream with a fork, managing to drop quite a bit on the table cloth. He ended the meal by blowing his nose loudly on his linen napkin. Emma had giggled all the way through the meal, much to her mother's fury.

"I just had to escape, dear girl," she said in her wonderfully theatrical way. "And what did you do over the holidays? What secrets do you hide behind that innocent façade? Tell, tell."
I blanched and then blushed and must've looked so confused that she laughed.

"Oh, my giddy aunt, you have been up to something, naughty girl. Are you going to tell?"

"I'm blushing because I've been so boring ... studying all the time ... and you've had all this fun and games."
I'm not sure she was convinced, but she was a good friend and never pried. And we were both distracted by Morag's bumbling entrance as she fell over her bags into the flat.

"Anyone want to buy an elephant?" said Emma. And we all laughed.
We fell back into our easy routine and life continued although both girls mentioned on several occasions that I was much quieter. This was hardly surprising as I was still bleeding heavily and did not feel inclined to horsing around or all-night partying. The usual cure-for-all-ills, a trip to the Chocolate House, was suggested and we set off down Princes Street in pursuit of Deep Purples and Knickerbocker Glories. I was really enjoying the chat and the ice cream when a small baby at an adjoining table started to cry plaintively. I felt a warm trickle from my breasts and bolted to the ladies. I locked myself in and sat there with tears running down my face and milk running down my clothes. Emma and Morag came looking for me. I came out of the toilet cubicle, made a beeline for the wash-hand basin and splashed water on my face, deliberately soaking my blouse so that the milk stains would be camouflaged. After that I bound up my breasts at night and cut down drastically on my fluid intake. This meant I had headaches a lot but it solved the problem of the milk

Mick graduated from his counselling course that June and he and Molly married that summer. It was a tremendous bash with all the money a bookie could lavish. It took place in the little chapel in Rosyth which was beautifully decorated with flowers for the occasion. Molly was truly lovely in a ballerina-style white dress and long veil held in place with a dainty tiara of pearls. She carried a bouquet of yellow rosebuds and long trailing maidenhair fern intertwined with fine satin ribbons that spilled down her dress like spring flowers in the snow. Her eyes were shining and her face full of a radiance I had never seen in her for many a day. I was so happy for the pair of them that I cried all the way through the service and looked an absolute sight in the photographs.

After the ceremony and the photographs we all went to a hotel to eat. There were nearly a hundred guests in all seated at long tables, resplendent with flowers and silver wear. Maryanne and Bridget with their toddlers were amongst the guests and everybody made a real fuss of the children. Even my father was so taken with his little grand-daughters that his anger against their mothers melted and he sat with one on each knee for most of the evening. I had never seen him tender and I couldn't take my eyes of him. The whole wedding was like a beautiful dream. Even mother seemed happier than I'd seen her in years. She was glad, no doubt, to see Molly set free to live her own life.

I have always been grateful that Molly's wedding was so magical because it was the last time that the family was all together and happy. The photographs became more than just a record of a special event: they became icons revered forever afterwards.

The dancing went on well into the evening, but
eventually Mick and Molly had to depart for the Ferry
to Ireland to spend their honeymoon in Dublin. I was
to travel as far as Derry with them where they would
stop overnight with Mick's parents and I would spend
some time with Mary. She had stayed at home to look
after her shaken grand parents so that her mum and
dad could come to Scotland and even stay for a short
holiday. During the dancing the happy couple had
slipped away to change and suddenly the band struck
up "For They Are Jolly Good Fellows" and they
appeared in our midst dressed in their travelling
clothes. While everyone else in the room gathered
round to sing and wish them all the best, I hurried
upstairs to collect my things and be ready for the
journey with them.

My presence in the honeymoon car was the cause of a
lot of good-humoured commentary which brought
blushes to my cheek. I felt a bit of a fool really sitting
behind the bride and groom with "Just Married"
scrawled all over the car in lipstick and shaving foam.
Then Maryanne's husband, Calum, shouted, "Did
they throw in the younger one to make sure you'd
take her big sister?" and I could've died of
embarrassment. An awkward titter ran round the
group waving us off. Maybe Calum's words were just
careless banter, maybe he didn't know the story of
poor unmarriageable Leah and how her father had
fooled her sister's husband into marrying them both.
In some way the story seemed appropriate to me. I
was a girl with a secret past which might make me
unacceptable to a lot of men. Most people there knew
the story of Leah - Molly and I certainly did - a
terrible tumult of shame and anger welled up in me.

"The man's got six beautiful daughters and I'd
like to have them all, so you'd better look out for your
wife," shouted Mick and everybody laughed, breaking
the tension.

"Women like men in uniform," Calum said. "You'd never prise her away from me."
He drew himself up to his splendid six-foot-three inches and I must admit he looked very handsome in his dress Black Watch kilt.

We roared off with the laughter still ringing round us and I knew Molly would always be happy with a man like Mick. As we sped along the summer roads the frothy verges of Ladies Lace seemed to have been specially grown there for our bridal passage and the waving green boughs of over-hanging trees made me think of the triumphal entry into Jerusalem on Palm Sunday. We hardly spoke, but the journey was relaxing as the warm aura from the newly weds cocooned them and yet sent out soft messages of love to me. I hoped one day I would be as lucky as Molly. When we got to the ferry Mick and Molly fussed over me till they felt I was completely comfortable in my little cabin before they went off to share their own and embark on the first night of their life-long journey together. Next morning we disembarked at Belfast and started the drive to Mick's parents' house where I would stay with Mary while the couple honeymooned in Dublin.

In Belfast Harbour we noticed that the RUC officers on patrol duties were wearing bullet-proof vests and carrying Sten guns. We thought nothing of this, however, because we had been brought up in a country where the police were always armed and the image of a gentle village bobby was the stuff of fairytales. In fact we didn't even mention it and we chatted happily about the wedding as the car bowled along with all the others from the ferry into the open countryside outside Belfast. We all marvelled at my father's sweet temper during the reception and, in particular, at his tolerance of the wild antics of the grandchildren. Inevitably this brought back memories of his lack of tolerance with our own childhood antics but there was no way that I was going to allow such thoughts to trail their clouds of gloom across our sunny horizon. I'm sure Molly felt the same. Maybe she had even forgiven him. She was that kind of girl. All I know is I am glad of those wonderful pictures of him that the wedding has left in my mind. Often since I have found myself thinking of them on the long slow climb up through Glenshane Pass.

It is the only place where I can evoke those few happy memories of my father. It is a really lovely drive where you climb and climb up through sheep and heather to 1000 feet and then descend in a wild free-wheeling hurdy-gurdy kind of way like a torrent rushing from the hills to the sea. From the top of the Pass you can see the lush green plains and forest parks spread out below and breathe the clean air of the Sperrin Mountains that makes you feel giddy as if you are perched on top of the world. Far away, at the edge of everything is a great wilderness of water where the Atlantic Ocean meets the North Channel.

Dungiven, the small town at the bottom of the Pass, was a bit of a shock to us after the beauty of the scenery we had just passed through. Its neat little High Street was a mess of debris and there was so much barbed wire round the police station it looked like a relic of the World Wars. We hurried through, intimidated and silent. This was the beginning of much worse things to come.

By the time we got to the sign "Londonderry, Historic City" we realised we were about to witness history in the making. The whole centre of the town was at a standstill and we had to queue with hundreds of other cars to get over the Craigavon Bridge which crosses the River Foyle in the centre of town. The centre was a seething mass of humanity. The British Army had just arrived in the city and it was engaged in the evacuation of the RUC. Many people had turned out to witness the departure of the RUC under army escort. They had never been a popular police force with the locals, and now the Troubles made their situation in the city untenable. They were constantly accused of being sectarian and even involved in promoting civic unrest. Youths were hurling missiles at them and cheering wildly at their departure. I wondered idly what my father would make of all this, believing as he did in Great British justice.

What I found strange was the way the Catholic population, despite fairly recent history, cheered the British Army and welcomed them as saviours. In 1969 the majority of Catholics in Derry felt the army would bring peace and there was a real sense of relief, celebration even, in the air. In the months previous to the arrival of the army, Loyalists had attacked a Civil Rights March from Queens University, Belfast at a small village called Burntollet, near Derry and injured students, a number of them seriously while the RUC, it was said, looked on. Personally, at that time, I just wanted out of the hot car and into a bath. But it took over an hour to get clear of the city and into the leafy suburbs where Mick's parents lived.

I had a bear-hugging reunion with Mary and the journey seemed worth the while. She had grown more confident - how much more I was to find out soon - and it showed in her manner and bearing and transformed her completely. She was, in fact, altogether lovely as she danced about me admiring my hair, my clothes, everything, even my nail polish.

"You'll knock them all dead!" she said. "Borderland won't know what's hit it when you arrive. Do you fancy going out tonight?"

"Give the girl time to draw breath, for heaven's sake," laughed Mick, "and put the kettle on before we all die of thirst."

Mary skipped out of the room to see to it. We were too tired after the hectic wedding week to venture out that night and it didn't seem a very good idea anyway

157

given the buzz of activity from the army. There were armed patrol cars and jeeps racing round the streets even in our quiet suburb all night long. My dreams kept verging on nightmare as the sound of patrol vehicles and soldiers' voices filtered through my sleep.

Next morning I heard a shriek from Molly and rushed into the living room. She had just jumped back, white-faced from the window. Gingerly I crept forward and peeped round the curtains. I, in turn, jumped back as if scalded when I saw two soldiers, in full camouflage gear with automatic weapons, creeping along the hedge at the bottom of the garden. I sat trembling waiting for a burst of fire. Nothing happened but Molly and I were still scared to leave the room. Then Mick came through and laughed at us when we told him what had happened.

"How are they supposed to protect you?" he asked, "If they don't hang around your house and carry guns?"

"I don't want to be protected. I want to be in Edinburgh where they don't need soldiers with guns," I said.

"It's the shops you'll be after," he laughed, "withdrawal symptoms already?" and he insisted on taking us into the shopping centre despite all my protests.

Derry is almost as beautiful as Edinburgh. The old city walls in mellow stone still encircle the heart of the city with their impressive archways where once the gates stood strong and there are some fine buildings like the Guildhall and the Cathedral. There are tree-lined streets with the River Foyle flowing at their heart. The wonderful shops round The Diamond rival Princes Street.

But the army turned it into a foreign place overnight. Now it was the sort of place you see on the evening

158

news with an armed soldier at every corner and
patrols walking through the streets, the last two
walking backwards so that guns bristle from all
angles. We were stopped, our bags were searched, our
persons were searched and our minds were raked with
questions. This looked like a very savage peace to me.
The shops all had wire grids over the windows and
many had racks of damaged goods at reduced prices
because of fire, water or smoke damage. Mary,
already inured to the horror of civil war, bounced
from rail to rail and picked up bargains. But I looked
on the city I had loved and wept.

CHAPTER 15

"Oh Danny Boy, Oh Danny Boy, I love you so"

The presence of the army continued to make me feel uncomfortable, but most of the people around me seemed to accept it quite quickly. I suppose so many things had happened over the past five years in Northern Ireland that its people had become much more adaptable than the rest of us and had learned to accept situations which would've outraged any other Briton. My elderly aunt had started making cups of tea for the soldiers who skulked along, bent double, on patrol under her hedge. The children coming home from primary school would ask the soldiers to show them their guns and scramble over Saracens as if they were climbing frames in the park. They talked very knowingly about the purposes and capabilities of various armoured vehicles. Shoppers submitted to having their bags searched without a word. Girls, even Mary, regarded this un-looked for influx of young men with interest despite the legendary stories of tarring and feathering which had taken place during the days of the Black and Tans. I was amazed and felt that somehow I had missed some important events that could explain this change of outlook. Which, of course, I had. Only the people living in Northern Ireland truly knew about what had been happening there. The rest of us knew only what the media chose, or was allowed to choose, to tell us. And so I had to accept that, contrary to all appearances, the presence of the army made life better there. But it was still with some misgivings, that I accompanied Mary later that summer of '69 to a pub over the border in Donegal. This meant crossing an army checkpoint and risking the ignominy of being searched.

We went to a pub that I thought I remembered. But when I saw it again I realised I had forgotten the long low building with the stout outer door. I had forgotten the strange thatched roof with its inset half-moon shaped windows that looked like frog's eyes. I had forgotten how it was tucked up a little lane between high banks of turf which the window-eyes peeped over as if the whole building could quickly duck out of the view of an intruder when necessary. It was a fantastical sort of place that you didn't quite believe existed when you weren't there. I could easily imagine that it was to such a pub that Aragorn came in his quest for the rings. Indoors, too, seemed to belong not only to another time but also to another world. The dark interior had a blazing fire at either end of a long low room even on this warm summer evening and the flames flickered in the grates creating tongues of light and wells of deep shadow on the rough walls and the bare wooden floor. The dim overhead lights spoke of kings with their strange crazed-glass balls held by crowns of brass and I thought again of Aragorn and the Lord of the Rings. The warm, friendly atmosphere soon dispelled such thoughts, however, and the fiddle music immediately set my feet tapping. I found myself dancing to the bar where an old man playing the spoons gave me a lovely toothy smile and clacked the spoons like silver castanets. They flashed against the back of his hands, on his forearms, on his thighs and even on his head so that the eye as well as the ear was enthralled. The bar was crowded with people from Derry in search of good craic and respite from the Troubles. Alcohol was flowing freely and a good deal of laughter and backslapping was going on. Mary threw herself into the proceedings with gay abandon, starting off with a long vodka and a quick look around to eye up the talent. Every couple of minutes she seemed to see somebody she knew and would shriek, "Sheila, how are you doing?" or "How's the form, Bridie?" across the crowded room. Most of these girls turned out to be student nurses with whom she worked and shared accommodation. We eventually joined a group of them and got high on a cocktail of booze, hormones and youth. We were young and sexual and the talk never strayed far from men.

"Isn't he a dote?" Mary asked, digging me in the ribs and nodding towards a young man standing at the bar. "I wouldn't mind a roll in the hay with him," she was saying when she noticed my mouth had dropped open.

There, older, broader, handsomer than I had ever seen him, stood Pat Malloy.

"Hands off. I saw him first!" she said.

"Oh, no you didn't," I said as I rose and moved my shaking legs in his direction. I stood right behind him, placed my hand over his mouth as he had done to me once, took a deep breath before I spoke.

"So you got away again?" I said in a half whisper.

I felt his whole body go rigid for an instant as if terrified and then he turned round relieved. His face was a kaleidoscope of many emotions which he was trying to mask. One of them was fear.

"Yes," he replied almost inaudibly. Then with mock cheerfulness he rushed on. "I went back to the house, your aunt's place, but it was full of strangers. They didn't seem to know anything about you."

"She rents the house to Germans … does it through an agency … they wouldn't know."

"No, no, I can see that …" His voice tailed off. There was an awkwardness between us that smothered our heartbeats, neither of us knowing what to say next.

"I'd better get back to my friends," I said and turned to go.

"Could we meet after Mass on Sunday?" he asked urgently as I was walking away. I turned back, my face, no doubt, full of enquiry.

"It's difficult. I can't talk here," he said to my unspoken question.

"Saint Eugene's?" I asked.

"No, Massmount. Ten o'clock. You'll get a bus from the Lough Swilly Depot in the Strand Road."

I nodded, sensing some undefined risk, and went back to Mary.

"What was all that about?" she asked eagerly.

"Nothing really," I said, "I knew him once." But the laughter of the rest of the group rolled round me and past me as I turned his words over and over in my mind. Why Massmount? My own chapel was only a stone's throw from my door. Why not go there? I was mulling this over and half-listening to a conversation between Mary and the young man beside her,

"We were told not to fraternise with the locals," he was saying, "but it's hard to resist such beautiful girls."

"Aw, get away out of that," laughed Mary.

"And it's so lonely here. I mean, nobody wants us here."

"What did you expect?"

"Action, I suppose. Catholics and Protestants having a square go at each other"

"And you stopping them killing each other? And flowers for the peace-keepers?"

"I'm not sure. Not this anyway. Not this endless, mindless patrolling.

"It can't be easy for you."

"It's not easy to take the hostility. It's our own country, after all."

"I think you'll find that a lot of people wouldn't agree with you there," said Mary.

"Penny for them." said an English voice close to my ear and, suddenly startled, I spilled my drink down the front of my dress.

"Sorry, oh, damn, I'm so sorry," said the voice and a hairy male hand was wiping the front of my dress and its owner was muttering apologies.

"Don't," I said and grabbed the hand, more tightly I suppose, than his action warranted, narked at the intrusion into my thoughts.

"Ok, Ok, I'm not going to touch you up or anything," he said testily and I freed his hand and looked up into a very handsome, sunburnt face.

"Just leave it," I said. "It'll wash out."

"I'll get you another drink, then. What will you have?"

"Nothing. It's fine."

"But I insist," he was saying when a huge hand grasped him by the shoulder.

"You heard the lady. Piss off and leave her alone."

I froze as I recognised the harsh timbre of the Northern voice. I didn't dare look up in case I betrayed my knowledge. And I didn't want to be able to put a face to that voice.

"Ok, Ok! I'll be off," said the other.

"You're off already," said the Northerner. "I could smell you from the other side of the room. I could smell out a limey anywhere. Just you remember that!"

Only then did I really take notice of the fact that all the young men who had joined Mary and her friends were soldiers and their accents and short hair made them stick out a mile from the rest of the company. I was seized with a sudden shivering sensation that Pat's presence in the bar was somehow connected to them. I looked involuntarily to where he had been, but he was no longer there.

"Let's go, Mary," I said standing up.

164

"Don't be silly. The evening's only half gone. Never mind big mouth, Eamon." She turned to Eamon as she spoke. "Bog off!" she said.

"There's ways of dealing with girls who hang out with soldiers," he said menacingly and a cold fear settled in my stomach.

"Away and play with yourself," she said defiantly and I was terrified for her. She stroked the face of the soldier sitting next to her and said, "You're gorgeous, I can't blame the local boys for being jealous."

Next minute the soldier was out cold as Eamon hit him between the eyes with his huge fist. The table overturned as he fell and a great rumpus broke out as suddenly everybody joined in the fray. I grabbed Mary's hand and made a run for the door. At the same moment I saw Pat grab Eamon by the scruff of the neck and drag him out of the fight.

"You bloody idiot," he was saying as he dragged him away.

Once outside we were at a loss as to what to do next. We had cadged a lift to Dunleary's Den and had no idea how to get back except by doing the same. The pub was not on a regular bus route. In fact, there were no regular bus routes in that part of Donegal. We would, therefore, just have to sit on the wall outside till others from Derry came out. Mary was giggly with alcohol and excitement, but I was desolate, fearing something terrible might happen to her. I looked at the deep blue summer night sky and thought of Emma and Morag in Edinburg. How simple and normal their lives were. At this moment in time they were probably in The Pentland singing patriotic songs along with The Corries with nothing at all to worry about. Later they would stroll home along Princes Street after midnight, still humming the haunting tunes and occasionally breaking into the lovely

choruses as we had often done. I began to hum our
favourite which was

"Come now, gather now, here where the
flowers grow,
White is the blossom as the snow on the ben
Hear now freedom's call, We'll make a
solemn vow,
Vow by the roses of Prince Charlie."

I was remembering how we would stop to look at the
displays of finery in the fabulous shops, and then take
up the singing again, enjoying the warm scent of
flowers wafting from Princes Street Gardens on a stir
of night air, completely safe in our nostalgic
recollections of Scotland's bitter history and
unscarred by care. At that moment I was desperately
homesick for Edinburgh.

Eventually a couple of nurses Mary knew emerged
from the uproar inside the bar and offered us a lift
back to Derry which we gratefully accepted. They
told us that if the soldiers at the border check point
asked us where we'd been we were to say we had
been at Borderland Ballroom. We didn't want to be
dragged in for questioning about the incidents in the
pub which the army would know about by now.

We were just pulling out of the car park when the
back door of the car was wrenched open and a man
piled into the back seat beside us.

"Sorry to intrude, ladies," said the
unmistakable voice of Eamon.

"Ah Christ, not you again," said Mary. "I
thought I'd seen the last of you for a while."

"You keep a civil tongue in your head, or
you'll see a lot more than you bargained for."

"Cut it out, you two," said the driver,
Shiobhan. "I've had enough for one night."

Soon a dazzling searchlight and red stoplights warned
us that we had arrived at the border check point. It
was like Colditz. The glaring lights shining straight

into our eyes made it impossible for us to see anything, even the soldier approaching our car. I was terrified. But Shiobhan said, "Don't worry, it's only routine. They'll just shine a torch in the car to see who's in it and then wave us on."

A soldier approached the driver's side of the car and Shiobhan rolled down the driver's window.

"Driving licence," he said. "Where have you come from and where are you going?"

Shiobhan handed over her licence.

"We've come from Borderland Ballroom and we're going back to our home at Culmore," she said quietly.

The soldier shone his torch into the car.

"You sir, what's your name?" he asked pointing the beam at Eamon.

"My name's Eamon Heaney, what's yours?" he said belligerently.

"Pull over there and come inside please, all of you."

"   Why the hell should we? It's our country, you know."

"Shut up, Eamon," said Shiobhan, pulling the car over as directed.

"Best co-operate," Mary whispered as we trooped into the army building, "or we'll be here all night."

"Great!" said Eamon furiously, "Allow them to act like conquerors. Fall in with their bullyboy tactics. They can't force the natives to like them but they can force them to pay lip service. It's got to be "Yes sir, no sir" to them, if you want a hassle-free life."

They asked us all routine questions about address, age, job and so on. They were excessively polite to us girls, but they were stern with Eamon, eventually taking him into another room for questioning. We had to hang about for over an hour waiting for him. When

167

he came out he was almost apoplectic with rage and the soldiers who brought him back to us could barely conceal their amusement.

We hustled him into the car as quickly as possible, spitting with fury.

"Do you know what those bastards did?" he said. "They took me into another room and then said they were due a tea-break and they just went off and left me locked in a room for an hour. The bastards were just messing about, showing their power. That's a favourite tactic in subduing the natives, waste their time, act as if you can't imagine they can possibly have anything valuable to do with their time."

"They might have been more friendly if you'd kept your mouth shut," I said.

"I have no wish to be friendly with an army of occupation," replied Eamon coldly.

We drove home in silence after that.

Next day Eamon called to apologise. He said it was too much Guinness that had made him so loud the night before. Mary was very understanding but I was not convinced by his story and wondered what he was up to. He wanted Mary and I to go back to Dunleary's with him, but I was having none of it.

Eamon had been at school with Mick and spoke to him as if he was an old friend, but I sensed that the feeling might not be mutual.

"I hear this wee stunner's your sister-in-law, Mick, do you think would she give a guy like me a second look?"

"I hope not," said Mick. "I wouldn't trust you with my old granny never mind a beauty like Grainne."

"I'd be a damn sight better for her than a bloody soldier."

"It's not the Dark Ages. A girl can go out with whoever she chooses these days."

"Even members of the army of occupation?"

168

"It's not an army of occupation. It's the British Army. And Northern Ireland's British whether you like it or not."

"I might've known better than say anything against the British in front of you. It's a wonder you don't join the bloody army."

"Now you're being silly. I just don't see the point in making trouble."

"No, you're the sort that would stand by and watch your country raped."

"I think you're being a wee bit melodramatic there, Eamon.

"It's rape!"

"It's idle talk that could land you in a lot of trouble."

"But we're all friends here," said Eamon with a tinge of menace in his voice.

"You never know who your friends are in a country like this," Mick replied.

That night the army vehicles screamed up to the house when we were all sound asleep. Soldiers banged on the outside doors front and back like battering rams. Mick was first to the door, pulling on a dressing gown, and was immediately hustled away between two burly privates. Ignoring our protests the soldiers systematically turned over the whole house, even getting Mick's old sick parents out of bed and searching under their mattress. They had ransacked wardrobes, throwen clothes on the beds, emptied cupboards onto the floors and looked likely to rip up the actual floorboards when the officer in charge suddenly stopped to listen to his radio.

"I think we might have been misinformed," he said and withdrew into the night leaving total devastation behind him. Mick returned soon afterwards.

"Eamon, I suspect," he said.

This was the beginning of the abuse of the army by unscrupulous people who had scores to settle. They just phoned the confidential army line and told them that they believed their neighbour, family member or anyone else they disliked, had a weapon hidden in their house. Then they could stand by and watch or sit back and laugh while that person's house was systematically turned upside down.

Next day was Sunday and we all rose early for Mass despite our close encounter with the army the night before. I packed my bags for home before I set off to keep my appointment with Pat at Massmount chapel. I did not tell the family where I was going, only that I had a visit to make and that I'd be back before bedtime. Mick, I felt, had some idea of my venture, but no one pressed me for particulars and I was grateful.

I had decided I would return to Scotland the following day, seeing no point in staying in a war zone when I had somewhere better to go. I begged Mary to come with me, but she wanted to stay and help Mick and Molly move into their new home. I often wish that I had been more persuasive. But I was naïve enough then to think that only a stretch of water separated me from that other country which I had, at first, so reluctantly adopted as my home.

When I arrived at Massmount I went straight in, pretty sure Pat would put in an appearance at communion time as he had on the earlier occasion. And so he did. This time, however, the weather was against us and we cycled in the pouring rain to a small cottage tearoom which we hoped to find empty. But when we got there we found it closed, presumably because the weather was so bad and it relied entirely on passing tourists for trade. We were in the wilds, we were soaking wet and we had nowhere to go. I was cold and miserable and wanted to go to the store at

Portsalon, but Pat was not keen. Eventually he pulled out a moustache and a pair of spectacles from his pocket and put them on. I was amazed at how these small things altered his appearance.

"My name is Pascal", he said. "I am French, but my accent is mostly very good. You understand?" I understood perfectly and did not even smile at his disguise which I realised was essential.

I love the store at Portsalon. It has not changed since I first saw it as a small child and I suspect it was much the same when my mother was young. From the outside it doesn't merit a second glance. It appears to be a huckster shop with cheap souvenirs in the window. The entrance is poor, rather like a back door and tourists will look around for a better entrance before using it. But when you get inside what a strange and wonderful place you find yourself in. By the door is a cabinet selling ice cream and a wall displaying old weathered out of date maps and posters. But your gaze will have already strayed to the many wares dangling from the ceiling. There are galvanised buckets, besoms, fishing nets, hurricane lamps and all manner of beach goods hanging from big hooks. There is a high wooden counter or bar over which the shopkeeper sells cheese and bread and tinned peas as well as whisky and Guinness and any other alcohol you care to mention. On wet days everybody creeps into the store to drink or eat ice-lollies and chat. It has a television which was the first one in the village and which is still a draw to many holidaymakers who do not have TV in their chalets or caravans. In the souvenir area sits an ancient black telephone for public use and outside the door and across a little alley is the toilet where there is a bath with a hinged wooden lid fitted to it. This lid is fastened down with a padlock, presumably to prevent clients from taking a quick bath when they nip in for a pee. This bath always held and still holds a strange fascination for me. But the most amazing thing about the store is the view. The small shop opens out into a fairly spacious lounge with panoramic views over Lough Swilly and the hills that surround it. It is, in fact, perched on the headland overlooking Ballymacstocker Strand and, lighted on a dismal day like this one, it must look like heaven from the sea. Because of the rain it was crowded when we entered and I could sense Pat's uneasiness as he searched the many faces there. We would not be able to talk. Can there be anything more dreary for two lovers than nowhere to be alone on a soaking wet day?

I had made up my mind to tell Pat about Patricia but this was not the time and place and in the end I kept my secret. We had only one drink in the store and then we set out again into the driving rain. I left Pat at the crossroads and cycled alone to Kerrykeel from whence I could get a bus to Derry. I left the bike lying outside the village Post Office as he had told me to do. I had no idea where he would spend the night, but I did realise that he was protecting me as well as himself by not letting me know.

It's a long haul by bus from Kerrykeel to Derry and then I had to get another bus to Molly's house. I was miserable and tired when I finally got back, but worst of all I felt the day had been frustrating beyond measure. To see, but not to be able to be close to Pat was unendurable. I went back to Scotland the next day not knowing if I would ever get the chance to tell him about his daughter.

Mick insisted on driving me to the ferry. He, too, was anxious to talk about Patricia but found it difficult to get me alone without raising suspicion. As soon as we got in the car he broached the subject. I was not ready for his first question.

"Would you like to see Patricia before you go home?" he asked. "We could easily pop in on the way "

I didn't know what to say. I didn't know what I
wanted to do. She was now three months old and I
was trying to pretend she didn't exist. I was silent,
unable to think of anything to say.

"Let's stop at a café and talk it over," he said.
"I'm sorry, I know this comes as a bit of a shock."
In the end he persuaded me to see her, assuring me
that the couple who looked after her did not know my
identity.

She was beautiful beyond the telling, full of big wide
gummy smiles and bright eyes that disappeared into
slits when she laughed. I could see that she was going
to be very fair-skinned like Pat. Her dark baby hair
had fallen out leaving her now with only little wisps
of blonde silk growing in. I felt foolishly proud again
as I took her awkwardly in my arms once more. I
found it hard to believe that I had produced this
incredibly perfect and beautiful creature. A deep sense
of regret told me that this meeting would make it very
hard to forget her.
Fortunately my junior honours year had only one
exam. I found it very hard to concentrate on study any
more. Often I would sit in the library with a huge
tome in front of me and my mind hundreds of miles
away in Carablah with Pat or just holding Patricia. I
could no longer feel carefree. A trip down Princess
Street had no power to cheer me anymore. I felt
totally out of place in the world of students which I
used to enjoy so much and longed to get my degree
and move on.

.

CHAPTER 16

"But if you come and I am dead or dying

Mary wrote to me often after I got back to Scotland,
sometimes great long letters and sometimes pretty
little cards. She seemed to be getting along famously
with Eamon which I found disturbing to say the least.
Apparently she often shared a lift with him to
Dunleary's and he had given up pestering her about
chatting up soldiers. Even more disturbing was the
news that Mary was now dating the soldier whom she
had made friends with the night I had accompanied
her there. His name was Paul and she was full of his
praises. Eamon had advised her to see him only in
Donegal as he felt there was a real risk that tarring
and feathering of girls who dated soldiers was about
to make a comeback. Did she ever ask herself how he
knew that? I tried to tell myself that it was none of my
business but deep down I knew it was.
For this reason I was glad as well as apprehensive
when Mary wrote to say that she was coming over to
visit me in Scotland in early spring and that I would
have the chance to get to know the famous Paul. He
was in one of the Scottish regiments and came from a
town near Edinburgh. There was no way I could put
her off anyway.
I met Mary in Waverley Station on a cold bleak
Edinburgh day with a leaden sky and the air full of the
threat of sleet. It was her first experience of the sharp
East wind and her first comment after greeting me
was,
      "Dear god how do you live somewhere as cold
as this? That wind is sharp enough to skin a body!"
So I decided seeing the sights was definitely out of
the question. I hailed a taxi and got her to my flat and
a hot cup of tea as quickly as possible. She was

desperate to tell me all the news about the latest sectarian murders, who was kidnapped and who was missing. I just didn't want to know and yet I kept listening, my heart thumping against my ribs, for Pat's name to come up. Mary rattled it all off like a litany as if it was just an everyday occurrence, which I suppose it was. I can't imagine what Emma and Morag made of it all or what kind of company they thought I kept when I was in Ireland. They sat open mouthed at Mary's news which they had no choice but to listen to because she was so full of such items as:

"You're wee friend Shaun, remember he used to sit behind you in primary five and nip you on the backside during morning prayers? He got lifted on his seventeenth birthday. They held him for two weeks. They had nothing on him. But, he must've told them something for after the army released him the IRA kneecapped him.

"Remember your man Paddy Hegarty? Well he was killed … caught in crossfire. Never did have much luck, God help him.

"But wait till I tell you this laugh. Grandad Friel's car got blown up! That old Ford that he thought the world of. He'd had it for over twenty years, washed it every Saturday morning without fail, talked to it even! Well Mick borrowed it – his car was in for a service – and he left it parked in the Bogside – and would you believe it – the army came and blew it up! A controlled explosion they call it. Poor grandad, he was sickened, really sickened. He'll never get over it. It was like losing a wean to him."

To me it was like listening to someone from another planet. How could anybody live through this and come out sane, let alone, laughing? How and when did people in Derry manage to get on with the ordinary business of life, I wondered.

To divert Mary from her litany of disasters I
suggested we go to see the new play at the Traverse.

"A play! It's a soldier I'm going out with, for
God's sake, not a scholar. I think a nice pub would be
a better idea. I want you to be able to talk to him."
I had secretly hoped that we might go to see a play
without him, but felt I couldn't say so. But I did grasp
my courage in both hands and bring up the subject of
Eamon in case we didn't get the chance another time.
I wasn't prepared to even mention what I knew about
the gun-running because I realised what a dangerous
thing it was to know and thought it best to keep it to
myself for both our sakes. When I got her alone I did,
however, suggest that he might be involved in
dangerous illegal activities connected with terrorism.
Mary just laughed.

"I'm sure all you people in Scotland think
we're all involved in gun-running, kidnapping, bomb-
making in Northern Ireland... But it's just not like
that. Even Paul seems to think that nobody's above
suspicion and he should know better. I mean the army
does know about these things. But, then again, Paul's
got reason to be paranoid, he's already lost friends
and colleagues to the IRA. Remember that big bloke
who spilt your drink down your dress?"
I nodded but I didn't want to hear the next bit. I
thought I knew it already.

"Well he was murdered. Some bitch working
for the IRA lured him down a lovers' lane and he was
set upon and kidnapped. They threw his body in a
ditch. Eamon was lifted for it, but they soon let him
go. He doesn't have the guts to get involved in
something like that for a start. Remember what a wee
coward he was at school? Remember how we used to
call after him 'cowardy custard, cowardy custard,
eating bread and mustard!' And he used to run home
crying to his mammy?"

I remembered how he used to rob birds' nests and pull the wings of butterflies. But my heart sank into my boots because I could see that she wasn't going to listen to me.

We met Paul in Rose Street where there were thirteen pubs to choose from. It was a favourite haunt of students and low life in those days and could always be relied on to provide a colourful slice of Edinburg life. After exams it was a student ritual to "do" Rose Street which meant spending an evening visiting every pub and having at least one drink in each. I was an infrequent visitor to pubs and, therefore, I never failed to be struck by the complete change in atmosphere and human behaviour as soon as the threshold was crossed. This one was warm and inviting and dimly lit with soft coloured lights. I could imagine a fairly civilised underground race living in accommodation such as this and I felt like a welcome stranger in another world where the culture was different from my own. Paul was very gallant and insisted on buying all the drinks. He was good-looking and knew it, but in a rather touching, naive way. He didn't flirt or eye up other girls but he did like to cut a dash striding across the floor to the bar and was a little more attentive to us and a little bit louder than I felt was entirely necessary. He completely charmed Morag who fluttered her lashes at him all night. With me he assumed an intimacy which I did not feel appropriate. I'd met him only once before and that had been briefly, on the fateful evening in Dunleary's Den. Yet we were still on our first drinks when he was saying to me,

"Not got a boyfriend yet?"

"Nobody special," I said.

"Playing the field, eh?"

"Not really," I said, beginning to feel uncomfortable.

"You mean you've not got anybody? A good looker like you? Proves what they,"

"What do they say?" I asked trying to sound interested.

"Men don't like clever women."
Clever women don't like stupid men, I thought to myself. But I didn't say it.

"That's why he goes out with me," said Mary and I had to laugh.
Realising that she could make us laugh, Mary regaled the company with tales of our days at the convent school. Tears ran down our faces as she told her version of our first night boarding together. We got more and more helpless with giggles. She got more and more excited and positively shouted when she got to the bit about, "No hanging out of the window naked except on Sundays," Suddenly the whole bar was silent and everybody was looking over at our table. We were silenced too for an instant and then we exploded with laughter.
Paul enjoyed the evening so much that he insisted on ringing up a few of his mates who were also home on leave that weekend. He said we were far too much fun to keep all to himself and his friends would never forgive him if they ever found out. We all went off to the pictures. I had a little twerp who kept trying to get fresh and brought out the haughty duchess in me. I heard him speaking to his friend at the end of the evening and had a secret smile to myself.

"How did you get on with yours?" he was asking. "I couldn't get anywhere with mine."
Emma got a really nice bloke but she wasn't interested, having eyes only for her vet, but Morag hit it off with Paul's friend, Richard, and they started dating. So all in all Mary's visit was deemed a success by us all and my flat mates invited her to come back any time.
But Mary never came back.

Some dreadful fate overtook them on their homeward journey. Their car was found abandoned outside Magherafelt on the road between Belfast and Derry. Paul's body was in the car. He had died from a single bullet wound to the head. Mary was missing and has never been seen or heard of since. There seems little doubt that the IRA were involved, but no-one has ever admitted responsibility and there was much idle speculation in the tabloids suggesting Mary was the murderer. Every one of us who knew Mary realised this was a smear campaign to hide the real criminals but we did not know where to begin to sort it out. It was also more important to devote all our energies to finding Mary.

In the early days we were sure she was alive and wandering about the countryside in a state of shock. Magherafelt is on the edge of a huge sparsely inhabited area of forests and mountains and a lost person could wander there forever without meeting another soul. Her family and friends in Ireland spent every hour they could combing miles and miles of countryside around the area in which the car had been found. But to no avail. Then they thought she might have been picked up by a passing motorist and they issued photographs and pleas through newspapers and television. But no response came. They also targeted the mainland in case she had been picked up by a car going to the ferry and had crossed back over the water. So far all enquiries have drawn a blank. As the passing weeks have turned into months we are less hopeful of finding her alive.

On Mick's express wishes I kept out of all the investigations about Mary. He thought it far safer for me to do so. Paul's broken-hearted family appeared on national TV and all my instincts made me want to visit them and offer them what comfort I could. But I didn't. Mary and Paul had left for the ferry from his parents' house and no mention was ever made of their connection with me or my friends. Mick thought we should keep things that way. Hard as it was I agreed with him. I could not involve my friends or family when it wasn't going to help Mary, but might harm them.

Emma and Morag and I talked about the terrible affair hour after hour, day after day. It ate up our lives. Morag was so scared that she stopped writing to Richard who had become her boyfriend. He was still serving in Northern Ireland. And gradually, as soon as she decently could after graduating, she stopped seeing me. I couldn't blame her.

CHAPTER 17

"If I am dead, as dead I well may be"

About three months after Mary's disappearance, the
biggest item on our social calendar for the summer
term, the May Ball, was imminent. Emma was
determined that we would go in a sixsome as in
previous years. I think she felt it would be a good way
of getting back to living our lives. Emma had her vet,
Morag had invited a shy boy from her Old Norse class
and I was now under pressure to find myself a partner
for the evening. The Ball promised to be a great
occasion, with Alan Price and Georgie Fame amongst
the entertainers and I desperately did not want to go.
How could I dance with Paul dead and Mary lying
God knows where? I had no one to go with either. All
that side of my life was on hold and I wondered if I
would ever get involved romantically again. I wasn't
interested in anyone and I thought this would provide
me with the perfect excuse for not going. Then Emma
had the brilliant idea of asking a priest we knew to
accompany me. Father Reid had come to study in
Edinburgh from the Cameroons where he had served
as a missionary. He was a really attractive man and
we all thought he was wasted being a priest. But
because he was a priest we never thought of him in
any other way. We would all go for coffee or to the
pictures together and he was a lovely, understanding
friend. He taught us all to ice skate at Murrayfield and
to sing folksongs to his guitar. He soothed over
squabbles between us and seemed very wise and
completely serene. For this reason, as much as his
position, we always referred to him as father.
He was delighted to accept my invitation to the ball
and I thought I could spend a pleasant enough evening
in his company. But I was dumbstruck when he

arrived to pick me up. I had only ever seen him in his crimson-girdled, flowing black soutane which we referred to as his frock. Now he stood before me looking like Sean Connery in an elegant tuxedo and a very suave hair cut, proffering an orchid. I suppose it was a bit foolish of me, but I expected him to turn up in his soutane. He looked so different that I saw him, for the first time, as a man and felt suddenly very shy of him. "You look great," was all I could manage before I shot into the flat in front of him.

"Wow Wee! You look terrific," said Emma.

"My frock's in the wash" he said. "This was all I could find." Turning to me, he asked, "Will I do?"

"You look fine," I said, deliberately avoiding his eyes, pretending I was struggling to pin the orchid on.

"Here, let me do it," he said and came over and pinned the orchid to my dress. I was painfully aware of my cleavage and the touch of his hand against my bare neck. As the evening progressed and the bubbly went to my head I lost my initial shyness and became relaxed, as was usual, in his company. I even agreed to call him Harry when he said he found "Father" a bit awkward in the circumstances. Perhaps it was the combination of chandeliers and crystal sparkling in the lights, exotic flowers filling the rooms with their heavy scent and the deep mellow music which created a kind of surreal atmosphere. Perhaps it was escapism from the months of weeping for Mary. Whatever it was, I felt as if I was living in a fairytale rather than the real world. I danced every dance and was breathless and flushed with exercise and excitement. Harry had a natural sense of rhythm and was a great dance partner, whether whirling me round the floor in a wild reel or waltzing to a moody blues tune. He seemed so sophisticated and dashing.

Like Mr Rochester, I thought. I never wanted the fairytale to end.

But "Auld Lang Syne came inevitably and it was time to go home. Harry fetched my coat and ordered a taxi. My bubble burst. I half expected his tuxedo to turn into a soutane on the way. When we got back to the flat he came in for a nightcap and chatted affably as he had so often done in the past. But somehow things had changed between us. I felt I wanted to distance myself a little now that the ball was over and was glad when the others returned, full of good wine and high spirits. We talked into the small hours because we were too hyper to sleep. Then Emma made the daft suggestion that we all climb Arthur's Seat and wash our faces in the May dew. It was 5 am as we trooped through the streets, silent except for the dawn chorus. Emma and Morag's guys had crashed out by then, but Harry, Father Reid, came with us which turned out to be a blessing. We made it to the top before our high spirits ran out, Then we were so flat we would've lain down and slept on the hillside if he hadn't been there to get us home. He coaxed and jibed and challenged us all the way. At the main door of our flat he kissed us each on the forehead and turned away towards his own abode. For the next couple of days I felt really serene from exhaustion, asking no more of life than a soft seat and warm food. I thought if I could dance like that every couple of weeks I would always be contented.

By the Monday morning Morag and I had recovered sufficiently to get ourselves out to lectures, but Emma still felt and looked peaky. This caused me some concern as she was the liveliest of the three of us and so I persuaded her to see a doctor since her final exams were only just over a month away. We had arranged earlier to meet Harry for lunch at the Catacombs so Emma said she would meet us there later. We were already seated and drinking coffee when she arrived. I moved up to make room for her asking,

"Well? What's the news?"

Emma looked at the priest first and then at me.

"Hold on to your seats," she said, "I have earth-shaking news." She paused dramatically, but I think we had all guessed what it was before she said,

"I'm pregnant! Oh, my giddy aunt, me a mother! Can you imagine it?"

Morag and I were dumbstruck, but for different reasons. I was amazed that she was so unperturbed. Morag, I think, was a little shocked.

"What will your mother say?" was my first question.

"She'll go mad, I expect, but she'll get over it."

"Does the dad-to-be know?" asked Morag.

"Yes, I went to see him first before I came here. He's absolutely delighted, which is just as well since it was his bloody fault."

"How come?" asked Morag, a little voyeuristically.

"Wined and dined me on Valentine's Day. Got me completely blotto! That's how."

"Dirty devil," said Morag embarrassed, but trying to make light of it.

"It's the most natural thing in the world," said Father Reid and we all stared at him.

"A very enlightened view for a priest," I remarked, remembering the many sermons on chastity I had been subjected to from priests in my school days.

"I'm a man as well as a priest," he said. "I can understand how these things might happen. So are you going to get married?"

"You wouldn't be asking that question if you knew my mother. I'm not going to tell her till after the exams. It's the only way I'll get peace to study. She'll start arranging everything as soon as she finds out."

"I could marry you here and save you all the hassle," he said.

"Lovely idea," said Emma, "but my mother would never forgive me. She'll want a big bash with hats and tailcoats and photographs."

"You can marry me," said Morag.

"I'd love to," he said, but I've set my heart on another."

We all laughed.

"It's bound to happen quite soon," he said.

"What?" We were all equally puzzled.

"Why marriage for priests, of course. It'll come soon. They'll have to allow it because the number of recruits to the priesthood is falling off dramatically."

We all stared at him as if he had suddenly sprouted horns. I thought of how often he had held my hand to guide me round the ice rink and how closely he had held me on the dance floor and I mentally shrank from him. He may have sensed our uneasiness for he quickly changed the subject.

"Will I get an invite to the wedding?" he asked.

"As long as you don't come in your frock. I don't want mummy's favourite minister feeling upstaged."

"It's a deal," he said. "Would a kilt do?"

The talk then turned to what we were all going to wear to Emma's wedding, and where she should honeymoon and where she would live when married. The pregnancy was forgotten for the moment. It was no big deal.

Morag and I spoiled Emma from that day till the end of term, bringing her tea in bed in the mornings, insisting she did not lift or carry anything heavier than a cushion and buying little items for the baby. Instead of going to The Chocolate House for a treat we went ogling lovely baby things. We bought striped bobble hats and dungarees in bright primary colours for the baby instead of the usual pretty matinee jackets and bonnets in soft pastel shades. We giggled a lot at the huge maternity bras and trousers with immense expandable waists. "Anyone want to buy an elephant?" became our catch phrase because Emma was beginning to look pregnant and said she felt like an elephant although she knew she looked more like a toad. It was as if the three of us were having the baby and not just Emma. Oddly enough, I really enjoyed that time of preparation for her baby despite the misery of my own experience of pregnancy. It was as if the two events took place in different worlds. I needed to spoil my friend because of the horror of childbirth which lay ahead of her that I could not bear to think of her enduring and felt constantly torn between enlightening her and keeping her in ignorant bliss. I suppose I also found it more bearable to focus my attention on the living rather than the dead. For in my heart I felt sure Mary was dead.

Father Reid came round a lot in the following weeks to keep up with the news of the baby and the forth-coming wedding. One evening Morag was out and Emma had gone to bed early and so we were alone together in the sitting room. We talked about how our student days were coming to an end and how different our lives would all be in the near future. I asked him how soon he would return to the mission after his degree. He wasn't sure anymore, he said. It depended on a lot of factors outside his control. He expressed his disappointment that the church had not yet made a ruling allowing priests to marry and he now knew that it would not come by the time he had finished university. He was, however, still sure that it would come sooner rather than later.

"In my opinion there isn't a hope of priests ever being allowed to marry," I said. "It would cause uproar worldwide"

"In that case, there's no point in my asking you to wait for me, is there?" he asked.

I knew he had spoken seriously but I was so shocked that I treated it as huge joke and laughed loudly.

"Am I so ridiculous?" he asked reddening. "The ball … it gave me hope. Did I misinterpret … we had a wonderful evening …"

"I'm sorry," was all I could say. I could not even begin to explain. I hardly understood myself why I burned with a deep inexplicable shame. After that I avoided him as much as possible and blushed when I was forced into meeting him face to face. My friends caught on to the situation quite quickly and were as appalled as I was at Father Reid behaving like a man. We even laughed about it. After all Shakespeare's men in frocks behaved like women and, to us, the priest had just been one of the girls. We all started avoiding him and he didn't get an invite to the wedding. With the cruelty of youth we forgot him and absorbed ourselves in preparation for Emma's big day.

It was the era of the hippy hat and we spent hours trying on big felt hats in many colours and shapes. Even the bride was to wear a big hat rather than a veil though of flimsier material. On the day she looked beautiful in her broad-brimmed hat and a long floaty dress with a leafy pattern in various shades of green. Morag and I found it hard to believe that one of the trio was now a married woman and we knew things would never be the same between us again.

The wedding was so exciting that it completely eclipsed the other great event of the year, graduation. Emma and Morag graduated that June amongst all the pomp and ceremony of an old university and, although I attended the ceremony, I felt completely out of things since I was not graduating with them and because it is essentially a family celebration. Both sets of parents turned up to applaud their daughters' triumphs and to lavish food and wine and presents on them at this very special time. And then they took them home. It was almost as if they were claiming them back after allowing them the freedom of the university years. I was desolate as I took the train to stay with my family for the duration of the summer vacation.

I got back to find that my bedroom was occupied by Mick's mum and dad who had come over for a short break at my mother's invitation. They had aged ten years since Mary's tragedy and she felt a break might do them good. I moved in with Kate trying to pretend that I always slept there, careful not to make them feel uncomfortable. But Kate had no such qualms and promptly dumped my stuff out on the landing, protesting that she was not sharing with me. Reasoning didn't work so I had to bargain with her for peace sake. She settled on my favourite dress and I handed it over resignedly, although I must confess that I intended to steal it back when the visitors left. My father was determined to show the visitors the sights, especially the new Forth Road Bridge which he couldn't have been more proud of if he'd built it himself. He wanted to walk across the bridge with them so that they could see the wonderful view up and down the river. My mother was anxious about the strenuous exercise involved because the walk to the bridge itself was a good five miles from our house, and then the bridge was a mile and a half long, but my father was not to be put off. He was looking and feeling good. He had been invalided out of his job at Rosyth Dockyard, but certified fit for light work and had already obtained a position, on condition that he passed a routine medical examination. The medical was the following morning and maybe he felt the walk would increase his fitness. Whatever the reason, he was determined to go. My mother was worried and asked me to go too and look after him. I willingly agreed. It would take me out in the fresh air and help me cope with the absence of my friends.

It was a fine clear morning when we set off. There was a veil of sea mist in the air, making it pleasantly cool for walking. The first couple of miles disappeared in chatter without our noticing. The talk was mainly about Mick and Molly. We were hungry for news about them and Mick's parents were eager to share it. We heard every detail of the new house and the lovely things Molly had done to make it comfortable. I could imagine her in a seventh heaven decorating and furnishing her own home although I'm sure everything would be overlaid with a film of sadness. Molly was not working because she and Mick hoped to start a family right away and meantime there was the house to get ready.

Mick had apparently settled in quickly to his new counselling job and was greatly enjoying, but he was still doing a lot of charity work which his parents were less than enthusiastic about. This was not because they were uncharitable people but because of the risks involved. In Northern Ireland there were Catholic shops and Protestant shops; there were Catholic pubs and Protestant pubs; there were even Catholic beaches and Protestant beaches. It's not surprising, therefore, that there were also Catholic charities and Protestant charities. Mick worked for a charity which was run by the Catholic Church but which did not recognise sectarianism. It simply gave help to those who needed it. At the time his parents were visiting, Mick was working as unobtrusively as possible in a Loyalist ghetto in Londonderry. His parents were afraid that he might come under threat from both Loyalist and Nationalist organisations who had no wish to see the community united even in poverty and need. I thought of Eamon and how their house had been turned over by the army. I thought of Mary and I understood their fear. My father, on the other hand, saw no reason for concern which showed how out of touch he was with the problems of his native city.

"The army will take care of all that, don't worry your head another minute about it, Dan," he said with his deep-rooted belief in British justice. And the sun suddenly appeared as if endorsing the truth of his statement. But soon the mist burned off and the sun became uncomfortably hot. By midday I was aware of it burning the shed where my hair was parted and my head felt too hot for comfort. I wished I'd brought a hat. Even more, did I wish I had brought a hat for my father who was red and perspiring. By now we were on a busy road and there was nowhere to sit down and rest. The only option open was to get him over the bridge to the hotel at the other side and refresh him there. The walk across the bridge was a nightmare of hot steel and exhaust fumes with no mercy from the blazing sun. I was all in by the time I flopped onto a seat in the hotel, so God knows what the older people felt. When we had rested a little and taken some tea and sandwiches, my father was keen to show the visitors round the village of South Queensferry and, in particular, the Hawes Inn which is mentioned in the famous novel, Kidnapped. He thought we could all have high tea there. He was greatly enjoying playing the host and showing off his little bits of knowledge of local history. But I vetoed the trip on the pretext that mother would have prepared tea for our return and would be vexed if we did not get home in time for it. I was, in fact, really worried that my father had already overdone things although he gave no sign that this might be the case.

Mick's parents were more than happy to head home and even suggested taking a bus, something I agreed to quickly before my father had time to disagree. I could not make out why he wanted to do all this walking anyway. It was totally out of character for him. The only explanation I could think of was that he was genuinely trying to entertain the visitors and take their minds off their problems.

Next morning he got up early for his medical. He looked very fit and well. His eyes looked bluer than ever because his skin was beautifully tanned from the previous days' walk. Although only fifty-five-years old his thick shock of blond hair had long ago turned silver and the lock brushed back off his forehead fell forward again shining like a skein of silken thread that had been cut open, the fanning ends catching and reflecting the light. He was very smartly dressed in pressed grey flannels and white open-necked shirt with half sleeves and seemed to be in a very confident mood when he set out although my mother told me afterwards that he had been complaining of a terrible headache.

He had a heart attack in the doctor's surgery and died later the same evening. I was with my mother at his bedside when he died. The rest of the family had been sent for and they arrived one by one as the evening wore on. Kate sat in the waiting room because she refused to sit by my father's bedside.

"He's dying Kate," I said.

"Good, save me going to jail for murdering him then, won't it?"

Only I was there with mum when the terrifying death rattle came and she threw herself on me and said, "Oh God, Grainne, what am I to do now?"

Live in peace, I thought. Find happiness.

"I'll look after you," I said and my heart sank with the burden of my responsibility.

CHAPTER 18

"You'll come and find the place where I am lying"

We did not wake my father as is the Irish custom. His body lay in a sanitised funeral parlour and the family went there to pay their last respects. It was the way things were done in Scotland and befitted a man who was proud of his Britishness. It was also much better for my mother since she was experiencing some difficulty in getting my father's body laid to rest in Londonderry. Apparently there were papers that had to be filled out and cleared by the army before he could be moved. A week after he died my mother and I, accompanied by Calum and Dan, arrived at Belfast airport with the coffin. The rest of the family had departed the night before by ferry. My mother was worn out with a grief that I could not fathom and the family were anxious to get the burial over in the hope that she could begin to put the death behind her. Although all the papers had been signed and sealed and approved we were held up at the airport for over two hours by the army. At first there was no explanation. We were ushered into a small room and asked to wait there. Even Dan had to wait although he was normally resident in Northern Ireland. The minutes passed, then the quarters and halfs till a full hour had gone. By this time my mother was weak with weeping and we were all very anxious about the people who had come to meet us at the airport. We didn't even know if they had been informed of our arrival. Calum was getting pretty shirty and hassling the soldiers on duty for information which they either did not have or were not allowed to divulge. He was really getting on my nerves.

"What's the hold-up? We have a right to know and I'm going to find out," Calum said again. This time he looked more belligerent as he moved towards the door. My mother was agitated. The last thing she wanted was trouble and Calum was a bit of a hothead who now seemed to have assumed the role of head of a family he hardly knew in the absence of other male members.

"I'll go I said, making for the door before Calum could do so. "Do you want anything, mummy?"

Just outside the door, a little way along the corridor, I saw a young soldier on duty and got within a foot of him before I realised it was Richard. He looked so different in uniform, less human, less vulnerable, I suppose. It was too late to turn away for he had seen me.

"Hello, Richard," I said. "I've got a bit of a problem here."
He looked at me severely and shook his head very slightly.

"What appears to be the problem, mam?" he asked.
I told him our tale of woe.

"Searching for arms," he said under his breath so that I wasn't really sure he had spoken. "Just routine, mam," he said aloud."

"Thankyou, sir," I said formally and walked away aware that I had made a gaff in recognising him. I went back and foolishly told the others what I had learned. Mother was wrecked with weeping already and did not respond, but Calum was furious and hell-bent on making trouble.

"Have they no thought for a poor widow? Hasn't she been through enough?" he was shouting. "I'll show the bastards what's what."
Dan assured Calum that he was needed by my mother's side while he and I went to see if we could

get Molly and Mick through from the arrival lounge to distract my mother for a while.

"Very unlikely," said Richard. "Security's pretty tight."

"But who would want to harm us?" I asked.

"I'm sure nobody wants to harm you," Richard said with ill-concealed contempt. "But they've got it in for our boys."

I wasn't at all sure who "they" referred to and said so to Mick's father.

"Can't blame him really. A lot of those young lads have been led down the garden path to their deaths by girls working for the IRA".

"Do I look like an IRA siren?" I asked. Dan shrugged his shoulders.

"It depends on who's looking," he said.

"Well? asked Calum when we got back.

"Just a wee while longer," said Dan.

"What a bloody dump," said Calum. "Your dad did well to leave it, Geraldine."

"You're right there," I said, "I'd hate to have grown up amongst all this."

"He didn't leave," said my mother quietly and we all turned to look at her. "He was given Hobson's choice; a job in Rosyth or no job at all."

"The bastards," said Dan. "They use a man while they can and when things get hot they dump him in another country like ... like ... toxic waste!"

"Maybe they were acting in his best interest," said my mother.

"You don't seriously believe that?" asked Dan.

"He did and that's what matters," she said quietly. "They told him that they thought he might become an IRA target."

"They thought they could use the excuse to get rid of a big family of potential Catholic voters, more like," said Dan. "You know what it's like here with

194

gerrymandering. Those in government in the North will do anything to keep their positions of power."
I had never heard Mick's father speak like this before and felt uneasy.

"Do people do anything but squabble in this God-forsaken place?" asked Calum.

"Yes they do actually," I said. "They have to get on with the daily business of living. You know, birth, death, work, the same as you," I was furious, surprising even myself with my outburst.
We all fell silent for a while and then Calum started again about the length of time the army were taking. Dan signed at him to leave it but he got more and more wound up.

"How long can it take to search a coffin, I ask you? There's not much room to hide anything in there. The body takes up most of the room in a coffin …" He stopped, a look of something dawning on him came into his eyes. Dan saw it and shook his head vigorously at him, but Calum blurted out,

"The bastards, the sick bastards, they search the body, don't they? They cut it up and …"
A scream from my mother tore the air. It was just like the one forced from my lungs by the torture of birth.

"No! No! No!" she screamed and I could not pacify her.

"Mummy, mummy," I kept saying, chafing her hands and trying to hug her rigid form. But she was lost to us in a nightmare world of terror and would not stop.
The screaming brought the soldier rushing into the room. My mother screamed louder and shrank from him into a corner. He moved towards her and she fell on her knees. Still screaming, she started rocking to and fro. Unhinged by the noise and the apparent threat to my mother, I threw myself upon the soldier, kicking and punching and scratching. I completely lost control so that the physical act of hurting took

over. I was a machine and could have gone on hitting him till I dropped of exhaustion. Dan had to pull me off and I saw Richard's face streaming blood as he hurried away. For some stupid reason I was glad that Morag didn't write to him any more and she would never find out the shameful thing I had done. As if that would make it any better.

Shortly afterwards an officer came and told us we could go. Calum held my mother and Dan had his arm round me as we were led weeping from the room to join the rest of the family and the relatives and friends who awaited us in the Arrivals lounge.

CHAPTER 19

"And kneel and say an Ave there for me."

Many, many people had turned up at the airport to see my father home. He had been one of six children and my mother one of nine. Most of the siblings were there with their grown families who brought children of their own. A long line of cars followed the cortege as it wound its way on the long road from Belfast to Derry where the body was taken first to Pennyburn chapel for a Requiem Mass. It had been our local church and because Molly had posted a notice of my father's death in The Derry Journal, it was crowded with old neighbours and acquaintances. It was a sung Mass and I knew it all, surprised that I remembered it from my childhood when I used to sing in the choir. The Dies Irae was so poignant that I wept openly, but less, I think, for my father's death than for the realisation of my mother's yet to come. I was also overcome with nostalgia for the strange, almost fabulous religion of my childhood.

After the service the funeral possession, now greatly swollen with people from the chapel, many following on foot, started out towards the cemetery, so aptly strewn across the barren hill at the top of the Lone Moor Road. I smiled wryly to myself as I realised the "lone moor" referred to the geography and not to some dark Ethiope who had somehow lost his way during the journey of the Magi and been doomed to wander desolately around a cold Celtic hillside for eternity: another mystical character was then deleted from my fantasy childhood world.

There were so many people that the Strand Road came to a standstill for about twenty minutes. I was completely bewildered by the turnout because my father had never seemed to have many friends during his lifetime and it was only afterwards that I realised that most of these people turned out as a mark of respect for the living rather than the dead. They had become inured to death in the ten years of the Troubles but understood fully the pain of the living who had to cope.

I understood this when we got to the cemetery. It was obscene with new graves. Dozens of mounds of raw earth and piles of wreaths everywhere pointed to recent interments as if there had been a massacre. Tricolours fluttered in our side of the graveyard while Union Jacks fluttered on the other side. For even in death the people of Northern Ireland are not united. I felt nothing but disgust. Never having given a thought to my own burial till now I was suddenly filled with the horror of being buried in a place like that.

Word went round in the cemetery that anybody who wished could come to Molly's house afterwards for a cup of tea or a drop of the hard stuff. And so during the remainder of the day I hardly had time to think as I plied an endless stream of visitors with refreshments. My mother insisted on helping and I allowed her to. After the incident at the airport she had become curiously detached and spoke as if her voice came from a faraway place: there was always a fractional time delay like the one you get on the television news when they are communicating with a correspondent on the far side of the earth. I was really worried but let her do as she pleased in the hope that being busy might keep her mind off other things. For my own part, I was desperately trying to keep my own mind off other things.

In the midst of death, life. On arriving at Molly's we had all been shown a little cloakroom to hang our coats in. I pressed myself against the wall in the hallway allowing my mother and Kate out before I went in to find a space for mine. But the first thing my eye took in was not coat pegs, but the big red sports bag lying in the corner. My heart stopped for an instant and I swooned. Surely Mick had not brought the baby home to Molly! With fluttering heart and heaving stomach I walked into the livingroom expecting at any minute to hear Patricia cry. I tried to imagine how she might look at fourteen months but could see her only as a three-months old, her age when last I saw her. I had thought of her daily since that last time but always as I saw her last: the gummy smile , the wispy strands of silken hair like a half-blown dandielion clock. My grief over Mary was mixed up in some way with grief over Patricia so that to think of one was to think of the other. And so I was engulfed by tidal waves of desolation and despair. No way could I face seeing my abandoned child at that moment. Desperately I tried to think of an excuse for bolting, was about to panic, forsake the sane world forever, when Mick came and put his arm around my shoulder.

"You OK, love?" he asked.

"The bag," I said. "Is she here?"

"Oh, Jesus, I never thought," he said. "I'm a bloody fool. I'm so so sorry. No, she's not here. Come in and sit down. I'll get you a drink."

"You look exhausted," Molly said. "I think you should lie down for a while."

The last thing I wanted was to be alone with my thoughts and so I insisted on helping in the kitchen and plying people with drinks. It gave me the excuse not to have to talk to anybody for too long. Eamon came to the house and insinuated himself into every conversation, watchful and wheedling as a weasel. He picked up fairly quickly that Calum referred to me as Geraldine, preferring to call me this name although all the rest of the family stuck with Grainne, despite Calum's frequent protests that "Grainne is bog Irish and unpronounceable."

199

"Geraldine? Did I hear you call her Geraldine? What's wrong with the good Irish name you were christened?" Eamon asked, turning to me.

"It's all right here," I said, "but in Scotland no-one's ever heard of it."

"Let them learn it then," he said, "instead of betraying your roots."

"Betraying …?" I began and then, mindful of the occasion and scared of Eamon's backlash, I turned to walk away.

"The young have to be allowed to adapt," said Mick, suddenly appearing beside me. "Sometimes it's the only way they can survive."

"Always the soft word Mick. You've got a smooth tongue in your head right enough. Comes from licking a lot of arses, I wouldn't wonder."
With that Eamon left the house.

During the course of the afternoon when the house was bustling with people, someone had nudged me and I found a scrap of paper in my hand. "The Blind Bridge anytime today," it read. When the house became quieter I left the company and the house to walk the few miles to my old village and take a look at my childhood home on my way to the bridge. The house now belonged to strangers who had tamed the wild front garden and cut down the big sycamore tree in the backyard. It was all very spruce and tidy, what my mother referred to approvingly as being "protestant looking." I was amazed at how small it was. In the picture preserved in my mind's eye from childhood it had been much bigger. But today I didn't have time to ponder this mystery. Instead I hurried past towards the unapproved road that led to the invisible border.
As a child I had been mystified by the existence of a border I could not see, thinking it must be a magical place like Narnia that only certain people could find.

It occupied the same space in my imagination as the wild goose chases my father sent us on, on Saturday mornings after he had been drinking. Molly hated Saturday mornings when my father sent her with all the younger children to the shop over the border. "Another of his wild goose chases," she would complain petulantly. I loved them even though I rarely saw a goose. We would run about looking for birds' nests or gathering berries or wild flowers, depending on the time of year. And the shop over the border sold the biggest and yummiest ice creams you ever saw. They were striped green, white and orange and as big as your fist.

I realise now that by the time I was seven I was adept at smuggling. My mother, who would've skinned us alive if she ever caught us lying or stealing, had no scruples at all about cheating the excise men because, as she put it, "God didn't make the border." To be fair, our nearest shop was over the invisible border and it was safer and cheaper sending us children along a quiet country road to get groceries than sending us by bus into the city. But this doesn't explain the sense of triumph that pervaded the whole house every time goods were unloaded from hidden places in our clothing or the deep well of the pram after a foray over the border. The roads around the village were patrolled by custom and excise men, known locally as "the water rats" and outwitting them was a source of great pride to those of us whose homes were perched precariously between the North and the Republic.

My first encounter with a water rat came when I was only about seven. Till that time I had a mental picture of them which was largely based on Ratty from The Wind In The Willows They were the baddies in the strange land over the border skulking about waiting to pounce on unsuspecting people who tried to bring stuff over from the south into the north. They must've been very powerful or in great numbers, I thought, because they could take away your bicycle or lorry or whatever you were using to smuggle things in. There was an enormous pound near Muff full of lorries and bikes and prams which the water rats had confiscated from people they had caught.

Our pram had a deep well under the mattress where goods could be carried and my mother sent me off one morning with Kate in the pram and a list as long as your arm to the store over the border. I had made the journey often in the past with Molly, but this was the first time I was to do it on my own. It was a good long walk to the shop and I was a bit apprehensive when I set out. But my mother assured me there was nothing to fear from anybody, not even the water rats, as long as I did not lift the baby out of the pram.

"Now remember, on no account lift that baby out of the pram," she repeated again as I set off down the path.

As I turned for home with the pram laden with butter, cigarettes and nylon stockings I felt very grown up. I was dawdling along singing to Kate and picking and eating blackberries when out of the corner of my eye I saw a dark shape moving some distance away. It was crawling down the road that I had to take. My stomach went slack with fear. Wildly I looked around for a way off the road, but the fields were boggy and criss-crossed with small burns and I knew there was no other way I could get the pram through. My mother would murder me if they got the pram and I knew I would never dare go home again if I bundled this mission and so I had no option but to brazen it out. I swallowed hard, said a silent prayer to The Little Flower and just kept walking at the same slow pace and eating blackberries. When I got to the Blind Bridge the sleek black car drew up alongside me and a smooth custom's officer slid out. He spoke differently to anyone I'd ever heard: a bit like the schoolmaster, but his vowels were funny.

"Where have you been?" he asked.

"Picking blackberries," I said. I could feel my knees wobbling.

"Have you by any chance been over the border?"

"The border? What's the border, mister?" I asked.

"You tell me," he said.

I tried to push past him but he put his hand on the pram handle. I felt warm pee running down my legs.

"Would you mind lifting the baby out of the pram?" he asked.

Of course! The magic charm! He couldn't touch me unless I lifted the baby out. Now I understood why my mother kept repeating it.

"My mammy said I was not to lift the baby out of the pram."

"Do as I tell you."

"If you want that baby out of the pram mister you can lift her yourself."

"You're a knowing little bitch," he said and got back into his car and drove away.

Now that cheeky, brave little girl seemed to be a character in a story which had nothing to do with me as I went looking for Pat at the Blind Bridge.

I was filled with nostalgia for those lost days as I passed the Redbreast Burn where Pat and I had spent many happy hours as children, filling jam jars with live minnows. When I came to the Blind Bridge I remembered how we had often dared each other to jump from the road, over the bridge to the field below. I sat on the bridge unconsciously stroking the scar on the middle finger of my left hand where I had once impaled it on a spike of barbed wire on the way down. I had been suspended several feet above the ground until the finger ripped and I had dropped bleeding, but triumphant, to the ground, the dare done.

"Truth or dare?" asked a voice I knew well.

"Dare, always dare," I said, turning round to look Pat straight in the eyes.
He looked much older and more care-worn than when I had last seen him. How could I begin to tell him about his daughter?

"Can we slip down here under the bridge?" he asked, obviously anxious to be out of sight. The Blind Bridge had no water, only a grassy tunnel under it. We climbed down gingerly, Pat first, stretching out his hand to assist me. How unlike our wild, heedless childhood daring it all was. As soon as we were safely under the bridge he took me in his arms. My heart was hammering in my chest and every fibre in my body wanted to twine itself in his. But at the same moment despair gripped me. I thought of the terrible secret agony I had endured as a result of our last lovemaking and I pulled away.

"I'm sorry," he said. "Forgive me. I'm forgetting myself, and your father just newly buried."

"It's not just that. It's so hopeless,"

"It'll not always be like this. One day there'll be peace."

"Not in our lifetime."

"Of course in our lifetime. It's got to come soon."
I shrugged my shoulders. I thought of poor Father Reid and his unfounded hopes of marriage for priests.

"We've got them cornered," Pat said.

"You're the one that's hiding," I said, "I never know from one meeting to the next where or when or even if, I will ever see you again."

"We'll be together one day," he said with conviction.

204

"In the grave, maybe," I said bitterly. "Most people of our age are married and thinking of raising a family."

"Ireland's my wife and my family," he said. "I am wedded to the cause."

"You'll not be interested in knowing you have a daughter then, will you?"

His face drained of colour.

"Oh, Jesus suffering! I didn't know. What can I do? What do you want me to do? Tell me what I have to do, Grainne."

"There's nothing you can do."

He took me to him and held me close till my sobs subsided.

"Tell me what I can do. Tell me how I can help," he begged.

"By not being a bloody fool. Don't get yourself killed, I sobbed."

"Where is she?" he asked.

"I don't know." Suddenly I felt utterly desolate. How could he ever understand what I had been through or why I had given his daughter away? But instead of the reproach I expected, he pulled me close and hugged me to him so tightly that I was hardly able to breathe. I could hear the hammering in his chest and was aware that I could feel every separate rib as they strained to cage his huge, bursting heart.

"My poor, poor darling," he said. "I have surely broken your heart, parting with your own wee baby. How, in God's name, am I ever going to make it up to you?"

"I'll survive. I always do." I thought of Mary. "What's happened to Mary?" I asked.

"Eamon's the one to ask that question off. But I suspect she's in the bottom of a bog somewhere in Donegal."

"Jesus, God, how can you stand there and say that as if it was the weather forecast?"

"You asked a question. I tried to answer it. Whatever you think of me you must realise that I would have nothing to do with business like that.

"So what business would you have something to do with?"

"I would only ever take out legitimate targets."

"Murder is never legitimate."

"Do they call it murder in a war?"

He was angry and I saw no point in arguing. Neither did I see any point in ever seeing him again. I had lost him long ago to the Cause, but only now did I see that clearly. I turned on my heel and walked away. This time again I intended never to look back.

CHAPTER 20

"And I will hear, though soft you tread above me"

Maybe because I knew my love affair with Pat was over, maybe for some other reason that I did not fully understand, I asked Mick if he would take me to see Patricia before I went back to Scotland with my mother. He said he would arrange it and if I wanted to we could take her out together for the day. I agreed to that as long as he promised to stay with me. I couldn't imagine coping with her on my own. The following Sunday after Mass we collected her from her doting foster parents. If they had any suspicions about who I was they did not betray them, but entrusted Patricia to Mick's care in a way that showed he was a frequent visitor even if Patricia's outburst of, "Daddy, daddy, daddy, on seeing Mick hadn't already given him away.

We took her to the seaside at Buncrana and I found myself having vivid flashbacks of my own childhood. Patricia loved the sea as I had done and kept staggering forward into the waves on her shaky little legs like a leathery-backed turtle which instinctively makes for the sea as soon as it is hatched. She got soaked to the skin and I was worried about her catching cold. But Mick just laughed and produced a towel and extra clothing from the car. How unlike my father.

When I was small the highlight of the summer holidays was a trip to the seaside at Buncrana. My father would have the whole house awake by seven thirty and Molly was detailed to whiten six pairs of sandshoes which were then put to dry on the kitchen windowsill. My father would inspect them and always find some fault so that they would have to be done again and we would have to wait longer for our trip.

207

Rosaleen was usually detailed to iron seven cotton dresses and several hair ribbons and they, too, were inspected for faults. The twins had to help my mother make dozens of sandwiches. My father's, which contained best quality cooked meats, were wrapped separately from ours. Eventually after much fault-finding and many tears we would all set off to walk to the head of the road for the bus. We had to walk in pairs in an orderly fashion or there would be hell to pay later. On the way to Buncrana my father always sat amongst us, surrounded by a bevy of neat well-behaved children. He would smile graciously at people who complimented him on his lovely family. On the way back, however, it was a different story. When we arrived at the wild open shore, even my father was incapable of holding us back and we used to run amuck in the sand and the sea for hours. Our dresses would get wet and crumpled, our hair ribbons would fall out and be lost and often we got scratched on rocks or filthy in seaweed. On the way back my father never sat anywhere near his dishevelled daughters and forbade us to even speak to him. We would sit subdued and hungry, knowing his eyes were boring into us from the back of the bus and dreading the inevitable row when we got home. I never ever remember him playing with us.

But Mick and I enjoyed having Patricia as an excuse to build sand castles, taking turns to search the shore for feathers and shells while she sat happily wriggling her toes in the sand. "Garden, she said, pointing to the sand. She stuffed handfuls of it in her mouth which horrified me. "Garden," she said pointing to the ice cream I bought her thinking it would make more attractive eating but which was soon covered in sand while she was eating it. She had a few other words like juice and kit(biscuit). "Daddy," she said to the ice-cream man."

"Now don't you go telling tales to the wife," he said.

"Daddy," she said to the wizened old toothless man selling donkey rides.

"I wish," he said.

Of course, Mick got called daddy most of the time and this seemed to delight him. All afternoon I was aware of the irony of this lovely little habit belonging to a child whose real father was remote and unknown to her. All afternoon I waited for her to say mummy, but it didn't seem to be a word she knew.

Before we went home we took Patricia round the shops to buy a few souvenirs. Everything delighted her. In a craft shop we went to there were carved wooden cats in all shapes and sizes with a great variety of facial expressions. Some of them were as tall as Patricia. She loved them. "Garden," she said over and over again and talked to them in her own special gibberish, cuddling and stroking and hugging them, quite forgetting that we were there or that anyone was watching her. I could have watched her do that all day. She was like a butterfly or a rainbow, giving the world something beautiful, but seeking nothing in return. The customers in the shop watched her and she brought a smile to every face.

Reluctantly I handed her back when the afternoon faded into sunset and it was time for her to go to bed. I knew there was no way I could keep her, yet for the first time I really wanted to. She had changed so much in the last year, would she change as much in the next? Would I be able to recognise her in a year's time? I didn't know the answers to these and many other questions and I didn't know how to find them. I decided, therefore, it would be best if I finished my course at university. That would give me a better chance of finding a good job and the money necessary to bring up a child on my own, I reasoned. How often do we make mistakes by considering the financial problems instead of the emotional ones? I regretted that decision for the rest of my life.

When I got back to Molly's house I asked mother how much longer she intended staying in Ireland. She thought she'd stay till the middle of August and get back for the beginning of Kate's school term. Kate was due to sit Highers in the coming session and mother was anxious that she would not miss any of the work. I wanted to get away. I could not stay so close to Pat and Patricia and keep my resolve not to see them. In any case I needed a job for the rest of the summer since I had completely run out of funds. Just before I left mother asked me to take home a huge pile of Arran wool and patterns with me to save her having to carry them. Mick's mum had got her interested in a knitting project to while away the winter evenings. I agreed to take the stuff but had nothing to carry it in.

"There's a great big sports bag kicking about somewhere," said Molly. "I think I last saw it in the cloakroom." She went to get it. "Funny," she said, "I could've sworn it was there only last week." She questioned Mick and it seemed that he hadn't seen it either. A search of the entire house failed to reveal it. Molly got annoyed. "Somebody must know where it is. It can't have grown feet and just walked out the front door!" We all laughed at her annoyance, except Mick who appeared concerned
But I never gave it another thought, sure that Mick had quietly disposed of it. And I would have to find other ways of transporting the wool.
Back in Scotland all the decent summer jobs had gone and I ended up working for a second hand car firm tarting up used cars for resale. I scrubbed and cleaned both the interiors and exteriors. Then I T-cutted the paintwork and blackened the tyres. The work was monotonous and uncomfortable. It got very hot and

claustrophobic cleaning the insides and the days seemed endless. Jessie, the permanent cleaner I worked with was a big feisty, heavy-bosomed woman who was really friendly and chatted incessantly about her family and private life. I didn't mind her chatter too much because it made it impossible for me to think about, let alone brood over, my problems.

I did mind one particularly sleazy salesman, however, who frequently hovered about our work area making remarks about our bottoms and loving to stare salaciously as we crawled into and backed out of cars. Jessie encouraged him, I suppose, with her ribald remarks about "backing in" and "jump starting." Once when we were having our lunch break she was sucking a whole tomato in a very suggestive way, pulling it slowly and noisily in and out of her mouth. He grabbed her, got the tomato out of her mouth and stuck it in her knickers. I was shocked and expected her to slap his face, but she enjoyed the tussle and I left my lunch and went back to work.

A couple of days after that I was busy in the back of a car polishing the leather seat. He must've crept up silently in his brothel-creepers and perhaps Jessie was in on the joke. Anyway I backed out of the car on all fours, buffing the seat as I went and I backed right onto the sleazy little pervert who had a hard on. He grabbed my breasts from behind and pulled me closer to him. I screamed and he laughed. I struggled, lashing backwards with my feet and he liked it. So I stopped. Then I grabbed his hand and sank my teeth into it as hard as I could. It was my intention to bite it right off if I could.

"You bloody bitch!" he screamed as he threw me aside. "Don't think you can get away with this."

"Met your match, boyo," laughed Jessie as he slunk away. Turning to me she said, "Don't take it all so seriously. You'll have to play along a bit if you want to stay in the job.

"I'd rather starve than allow every dirty little salesman who fancied it to paw me."

"He's not just any salesman. He's the boss's son."

"I couldn't care if he's the heir to the throne," I said.

The next day I got the sack. After that I got a weekend job in a Milk Bar. I slaved from ten in the morning till ten at night, cleaning, cooking and serving as necessary. I never stopped. But at least I was not troubled by men who think they have a right to grope women just because they give them a job.

But being at home in the empty house was very difficult for me and I will never smell rambling roses again without thinking of that time. The house and garden were full of the sweet scent of old-fashioned ramblers. Little white flowers cascaded over fences and sheds like waterfalls and spilled from jars and vases in every room of the house where I had placed them. Their perfume on those damp July days after my father's death was inescapable like my loneliness. I was not lonely for my father, but for Patricia and Pat and Emma and Morag and the life I should have had but which now seemed lost forever.

To while away the time I started to tidy my mother's house and sort out my father's clothes and personal effects before she came back. The task was so different from the time I did it for Uncle John. Then I had touched his things reverently like the relics of a saint. Every item of clothing that had been near his skin seemed worthy of careful handling, every cup and plate he used should have been put in a glass case like an icon. I put my hand in my pocket and took out his little briar pipe. I realised my whole life would have been different if I'd had a father like him instead of the mean selfish man my mother married. I rooted about on the top of wardrobe and I found the horrible canes which he used to beat us with. I tried to break them over my knee but they were strong and flexible and apparently indestructible. I lit a fire in the grate and burned them. I also threw in any cigarettes I could find. I thought if there's a hell he is burning there at this moment and I was tempted to actually burn everything belonging to him but refrained because I knew mother would mind.

My mother went mad when she saw that I had touched his things. I even got told off for stripping and washing their bedding. I wonder if she intended sleeping in it forever without changing it or if she was going to fold it away unwashed because he had slept in it. I could not understand her love for him and perhaps I never will.

I don't think the real effect of my father's death really had had a chance to sink in till she came home. Before the funeral she had been very busy and there had been people around all the time. Now she had to start the rest of her life without him. And because she had spent thirty years in his service she didn't know where to begin.

She would go to the shop for his paper first thing every morning, come back and make a cup of tea. Then she would sit down and do the crossword with her coat and scarf still on. I would find her still sitting there hours later, sometimes frozen because she hadn't lit the coal fire which was the only means of heating the house. Other times I would find her sitting in the middle of her bedroom floor looking through old photographs and weeping inconsolably. I had little patience with this. He had been a bastard to her all her life, why didn't she sing out her freedom now that he'd gone? Why didn't she throw aside her broken fetters and dance? Had she been too long a victim to remember joy?

She had never worked since they were married so going back to employment didn't seem even a remote possibility. This was unfortunate because she now found herself more hard up than she had ever been in her life. Despite my father's constant assurances that she would be all right when he died, she actually found herself penniless. In death he gave us as many problems to cope with as in life. The benevolent fund he had paid into all his working days refused to pay a penny to his widow. The small print said that to be a beneficiary the claimant's spouse must die within a year of the illness which had caused him to be invalided out of his job. My father had lived a week too long for my mother to receive benefit. Probably did it out of spite, I thought. I realised I was going to have to work part-time in my final year at university to help her and that after that I was going to have to get a job near home There was no question of sharing a flat in Edinburgh any longer.

CHAPTER 21

"And all my grave will warmer sweeter be"

With sinking heart I started back after the summer. I felt very old and responsible and out of touch with the other students. Emma, now happily married, lived with her husband in their home which bore no resemblance to a student flat. She spent most of her free time painting and decorating and planning the nursery. She was doing a teacher training course and Morag was in her class but never seemed to be around when I met up with her. Most members of my final honours class were study freaks and seemed to sleep in the library as well as eat there. I had no social life whatsoever. My part-time work as a waitress was my main contact with people other than my mother. Even Kate, now coming up for seventeen, I seldom saw. She had got completely out of control since my father's death and did what she liked. She smoked, drank alcohol and slept around, things I wouldn't have dared do at her age, or any age in my mother's house. She only occasionally went to school. My mother insisted that I try talking to her and I did.

"You're an old-fashioned virgin," she laughed. "Get real."

I was worn out by the end of term and although I was not looking forward to Christmas, I was looking forward to the break just to be able to stop for a while and rest.

The highlight of that winter was the birth of Emma's daughter in November. I was so happy for her. And so sad for myself. I wanted to spend hours with her and the baby but, naturally enough, so did her husband. I went to see her every day while she was in the

Simpson Maternity Pavilion and she was glad of the company and I was so happy to be intimate with her again. It was like old times. When she got home I started visiting every day but her husband made me realise quite quickly that three's a cloud as well as a crowd. I made myself scare till the christening the following January. It was a great celebration with splendid organ music, almost reducing me to tears when they played Robert Burn's "Bonnie Wee Thing". Foolishly I wished I'd sung a hymn while Mick and I were giving Patricia her DIY christening. Afterwards there was a champagne reception where I met Emma's in-laws as well as all her own family. The baby's arrival seemed to have put everybody on the best of terms, even Emma's new husband and her mum. I was aware of being out on a limb.

After the christening my terrible nightmares about Patricia in the sports bag returned night after night to haunt me so that I was worn out by lack of sleep even though I was on holiday and returned to university unrested.

A worse nightmare was to follow. It was on my twenty-second birthday that we got the terrible news of Mick's arrest. Since Habeas Corpus had been suspended in Northern Ireland, Mick could be held indefinitely without trial. I was completely wrecked by the news and very, very scared for him. So I set off for Ireland as soon as I could get a ferry. It was almost Easter and my lectures had more or less finished for the term anyway.

Molly was in an awful state when I got there. The army had come in the middle of the night and dragged Mick out of bed. They had only the flimsiest of excuses for arresting him. Apparently the red sports bag had been found and somehow connected to Paul's murder and they had traced it to Mick. Needless to say when they checked they found Mick's fingerprints on it. There were also a woman's fingerprints which they said could be Mary's. I knew they were mine. But it would be more convenient for the prosecution if they could say they were Mary's since she was under suspicion of murdering a soldier. I was consumed with guilt.

I confessed everything I thought necessary to Molly about the baby and about Mick's visit after the birth. I saw no need to mention Pat and she assumed that the father was "some contemptible free-loving student". I was amazed that in spite of dealing on a daily basis with terrorism she was still appalled at my moral slip. To her, sex before marriage seemed to be in the same league of sins as murder. Instead of lightening my load I felt even worse than I had before I told her my sordid secret.

I wanted to go immediately to the army and tell them about the bag. But Molly said this would be foolish. They would just arrest me too and say they'd caught another IRA siren. I was dumbstruck. I had every confidence in the legal system and told her so.

"You're not in Scotland now," she said, "This is the wild west."

I went to see Mick's parents and told them my story. They asked me to keep it to myself till they could discuss it with their lawyer. I desperately wanted to see and talk to Mick but they advised against that too. They told me it was becoming increasingly common for whole families to be held in suspicion and often the brothers of a suspect would be interned without trial in order to pressurise the suspect into confession. I knew I could not help Mick from behind prison bars and I agreed to be guided by his parents and their lawyer. We had secret meetings. But how secret was anything in Northern Ireland? There were terrorist moles working within the security system, there were SAS men who had infiltrated terrorist organisations, there were informers and double agents. There were even IRA men who would do deals with the RUC to rid themselves of their own members who had got out of control. I was prepared to do anything to help Mick, even die, I think. I would've agreed to anything that might increase his chances of getting justice. The lawyer said he would press for a trial date to be set for Mick. He felt my evidence was vital. It corroborated a lot of Mick's statements and pointed the finger at Eamon, as did much of the circumstantial evidence. While awaiting news of Mick's trial I stayed with Molly and tried to keep her spirits up. She knew Mick was completely innocent and yet she was sure he would be found guilty and imprisoned. I found this really hard to understand and just kept trying to reassure her.

"And I've not even a child to keep me company," she complained again and again.

"This time next year this will all be behind you. Maybe you'll even get twins to make up for lost time. Bags I get to be godmother."

"We can't have children," she said flatly.

"I'm really sorry, Molly. I didn't know."

"You're the only person I've told. I've been waiting for the right time to tell Mick. But when is there a right time for news like that and him so fond of children?"

I remembered Mick bathing my newborn and changing nappies, "I'll be a dab hand at this and Molly will think she's got a good catch." I remembered our day at Buncrana with Patricia. I understood her sense of desolation only too well. Even so I was surprised to hear myself say, "Would you like to meet Patricia?"

So many emotions fought for expression on her face that I was embarrassed to watch and looked away.

"It was only a suggestion, forget I ever said it."

"I'd love to meet her," she said firmly.

218

And so Molly and I took Patricia to the beach at Buncrana and had a wonderful day out. Molly loved her instantly and looked happy for the first time in god knows how many weeks. I was sad seeing how much Patricia had grown and changed in the past year. I had missed so much. By now she had had her second birthday: she would be over seven hundred and thirty days old and, in all, I had seen her on only eight of those days. She was no longer a baby. She was very steady on her legs and had developed quite a vocabulary. "Garden" was now used correctly and not as a generic term describing everything she found good. I was concerned to find that I was observing her in a somewhat detached way whereas Molly was completely wrapped up in her. When it was time to take her back Molly said to me,

"Did you notice her foster mother was pregnant?"

"I can't say that I did."

"How could you miss it? She was huge!"

"I probably wasn't paying much attention," I said apologetically and then wondered why on earth I was apologising.

"She could probably do with a break."

I knew what was coming next.

Patricia was my child. Molly was my sister. Mick, the fairest and most reliable person I knew was behind bars. Patricia came to live with Molly for a while, ostensibly to give her foster parents a break. Taking her from her foster parents was undoubtedly wrong and I have been paying the price daily ever since, but at the time she brought a bundle of happiness into some very sad lives. Not only Molly, but Mick's parents, too, were diverted by the child and they treated her like a granddaughter, buying presents, reading stories, offering to babysit: giving love. They especially liked taking her trips in the car because she loved it so much and was a great source of amusement.

They drove me into Derry one day and I was sitting in the front with Patricia on my knee. It was a rainy day and a lorry in front of us kept throwing up dirt off the road onto our car so that we could hardly see. Mick's dad pressed the screen wash and when Patricia saw the little jets of water spray onto the windscreen she got really excited. "Lorry doing wee-wee on our car." She laughed her beautiful childish laugh and clapped her hands in delight. Granddad was tickled pink with her remark. He was less enthusiastic about her humour on another occasion, however, when I was visiting with her. We were sitting in the kitchen with the back door open and she was trotting in and out between the house and the garden. Suddenly she came running into the kitchen looking very excited carrying a flute cleaner in her hand. She pulled at Dan's trouser leg "Come, come, " gramps come, big boo car make big, big noise!" We all hurried into the garden to see what had excited her. Before we could do a thing she had let down the third tyre of his car by sticking the flute cleaner into the valve. "Big, big noise," she said as the air hissed out.

We were absolutely amazed and could not begin to work out how or where she had learned this trick. I think she had found it out by accident. She was always sticking things in holes and I had already had to seal all the power points with plastic covers. She was full of surprises like that which made her a bit of a handful sometimes. But I wouldn't have had her do a thing differently because she was a constant source of surprise and joy.

But I had to leave her. My finals beckoned and I knew I needed to pass if I was ever to afford to make a home for her and also look after my mother. No date had yet been set for Mick's trial and it seemed unlikely that it would happen soon. I intended to come back the minute my exams were over. I went to the craft shop Patricia had liked so much and bought her a little wooden cat. When I was leaving I gave it to her and told her to look after it till I got back. With heavy heart I left Patricia with Molly and set off for Edinburgh.

I had missed out on a lot of work so instead of revising I was sometimes learning things for the first time. I set myself a rigorous timetable, getting up every morning and doing two hours swotting before I took the train in to sit my exam. I had a sandwich and a swim at lunchtime and then studied all afternoon unless I had an exam. I went home around teatime, ate and went to bed with my books. I would study till 2am and then set my alarm for 6.30am so that I could do my two hours before my next exam. I couldn't have kept this routine up for ever but over the two weeks I used it, it worked really well. I felt very alert and focused right the way through my finals. Afterwards I crashed out and slept for a whole day. I never saw my friends and indeed I hardly spoke to anyone at this time except when we were standing outside the exam hall waiting to get in.

As soon as I could manage I was back in Ireland. I was a good deal less focused about what I was gong to do there, but my instincts told me that's were I should be. I found in my absence Patricia had attached herself to Molly and had become quite clingy. It was understandable I suppose, but I was still very hurt. After all she was my child. I only wish I had asserted my rights to her there and then and taken her back to Scotland. How many such idle wishes have I made since? But, of course, it would've been really churlish to take her from Molly in the circumstances. I decided I would wait till Mick was released. Meanwhile I set about gaining her confidence again. "Where's the cat?" I would ask and she would bring it to me, placing it carefully in my hand and planting a kiss on it. Then I would say, "Clever girl. You've been good to pussy," stroke it and give it back to her. This became a little ritual between us.

The trial date was set and I was cited as a witness for the defence. I was apprehensive yet glad. Mick had already been too long from his family. I felt sure he would soon be home. I should have gone back to Edinburgh in July to graduate since the trial was still some months away, but because I couldn't bear to leave Patricia again I graduated in absentia. It hardly mattered. My best friends already had jobs and were engrossed in their own lives. It would've been only mother and me at the graduation ceremony and neither of us had much to celebrate.

No sooner had the trial date been set than Eamon turned up at Molly's house. We were both scared and unsure how to deal with him. Patricia was in bed when he came and we were glad of that. I couldn't have borne him to touch her. Unfortunately she woke up and I was forced to pick her up.

"Lovely wee wean," Eamon said. "And who does she belong to?"
Molly and I looked at each other. "A friend's," I said.
"Born the wrong side of the blanket, I wouldn't wonder," said Eamon.
I'm sure I blushed.
"Lovely just the same. You wouldn't want anything to happen to a cute wee girl like that now, would you?"
"What do you want?" I asked.
"Disappear back to Scotland if you know what's good for you."

"Get out! Get out, you evil brute," shouted Molly. I thought she was going to hit him.

"Now, now," said Eamon, "I was only offering you some advice."

I was shaking and I'm sure my face was ashen. Eamon put out his hand to steady me and I felt a cold shiver of disgust run over me so that the hairs stood up on the back of my neck. Perhaps he felt my revulsion for he left abruptly.

I handed Patricia to Molly and rushed into the loo where I was violently sick. We phoned Mick's dad and he phoned the lawyer and everybody assured me that it would be all right. Dan stayed the night with us, but I tossed and turned all night long and the old nightmares returned.

Next day the lawyer said he had arranged for Molly, Patricia and me to be placed under protective custody and we accepted. Although we knew we could not spend our whole lives in hiding and we couldn't imagine anywhere we could hide from the IRA we had no other option but to take what protection was offered us. When the two men came to pick us up I got Patricia's things together and dressed her carefully for the journey. My hands were shaking and my heart was cold with dread. I felt a terrible reluctance to step out of the house. At the last minute I turned back and made up some juice for the wee one. Then I decided to put in some extra towels. Just at the point of going out the door a second time I ran back upstairs and grabbed the little wooden cat. Patricia reached out from her place in Molly's arms, took it and smothered it and me in kisses. Molly put an arm round my shoulder and guided me to the door.

The rest is a blur of sound and vision. The noise of tyres screeching startled us. A car came careering down the street. A Saracen came roaring after it. An old man walking along the street with the aid of a stick suddenly threw the stick away and sprang towards us with remarkable agility, He was shouting frantically but I could not hear what he was saying above the noise of the squealing tyres. Just as we were crossing the lawn to the gate two men jumped clear of the speeding car and made off across the garden on foot. One of them was Eamon. The driverless car came hurtling through the garden wall. Then I was screaming with my legs pinned to the ground. The car was on top of my legs. Its engine was still running. I could hear it clearly accompanying my screaming. There was no other sound.

"Patricia, Patricia," I was screaming. But nobody answered.

I could see the wooden cat sticking out from a pile of rubble next to me. I couldn't see Patricia or Molly at all.

"Jesus, get her out of here in case it goes up." Someone was pulling and pulling at me. It was the old man. The pain was agonising. My legs were being ripped to pieces.

"Help me get her out, you bastards."

It was Pat's voice. The old man had Pat's voice. There was nobody else around.

"Patricia, get Patricia," I screamed.

But he just went on pulling and pulling at me as if his life depended on it.

I felt the flesh rip off my shins. The pain was unbearable. But I wanted to stay conscious. I wanted someone to get Patricia. Suddenly I was wrenched free. Pat lurched backwards and I was on top of him. He quickly rolled me over and lay on top of me and held me close, holding my body in a wild, desperate embrace. There was a great flash of light followed by a terrific bang.

Then silence.

CHAPTER 22

> And you will kneel and tell me that you love

me

> And I will sleep in peace until you come to me

.”

I became aware that I was moving horizontally through space, gliding on my back, feet first. There were figures in white and I was gliding between them at shoulder height. All around there was a strange ringing noise like machinery humming. I was in a kind of tunnel and there were lights at intervals above my head. I didn't know who I was. I didn't know where I was. Maybe I was dead.

A figure leaned over me and its mouth moved but no sound came out. I tried to move. Pain shot through every inch of my body. I uttered a cry but it was inaudible. The figure squeezed my hand.

Suddenly memory tumbled back. It came piling in, in reverse order, the explosion, Pat, my legs, the car, Patricia.

“Patricia!” I screamed but the sound didn't come out.

They gave me an injection and I passed out.

I am not clear about a lot of things after that. I remember being in a ward with cages over my legs. I remember silent, sombre visitors. I remember pain. I remember asking for news of Patricia and Molly and Pat but I couldn't hear myself speak. Once I was confused to wake up and find my mother by my bed. When I awoke again she was gone.

The person who sat with me longest through the silent nights was Uncle John. It was strange, when I was with him I could hear perfectly. He took me to a secret place over the border where I couldn't go on my own. It was a bit like the valley of the secret lake at Carablah, but the climate was heavenly and it was full of fruit trees. Patricia and Molly were there and they were very happy. They were dancing round a beautiful flowering tree singing. It was a laburnum tree and the delicate racemes of yellow flowers glowed against a navy sky studded with stars. Every now and then a meteor shower sent hundreds of these tiny stars floating gently onto the branches of the tree where they twinkled like fairy lights. On our last night together I joined hands with Patricia and Molly and danced and sang too. We were all wearing long white dresses. Then I saw Pat. He smiled his wide boyish grin and waved to me, but remained standing some way off. There was a scatter of yellow petals on his shoulders and on the ground round his feet. When it was time for me to go I asked Uncle John for instructions on how to get back there so that I could come another day. He said I wouldn't get in and I had to leave them all now and get back to my own world. I said I was scared to go back. And he told me not to be scared because Pat was my very own guardian angel and would be looking after me always from now on.

I awoke the morning after that last night with Uncle John to find my mother at my bedside again. She was squeezing my hand. I opened my eyes.

"I'm back, I said"

"Thank God," she replied.

Or at least I think that's what she said. I realised I was deaf. I asked for paper and pencil. She brought them and handed them to me.

"For you. I can't hear. You'll have to write the answers down."

She looked apprehensive.

"Where is Patricia?" I asked.

Her face contorted with grief and I knew the answer.

"I had her buried beside Uncle John," she wrote. "I thought you would like that."

I squeezed her hand.

"Molly?" I asked.

"Gone too," her lips said before she wrote down. "She died instantly. There was no pain."

I thought of the pain I had suffered with my injuries and I was glad of that at least. I buried my head in the pillows to hide my tears but when I felt my mother's hopeless hand on my back, stroking me like a child that cannot be comforted, I was touched with pity and made myself turn my face back to her.

"Pat saved your life," she had written. "Better love hath no man."

I knew then she had the whole story of my hopeless love for Pat and my secret baby. Knew too, that she had forgiven me.

I began to make rapid progress after that. They allowed me to see the papers, some of which were now months old. It was grim reading the accounts of my own family's deaths as if they were just news items but, strangely enough, it helped me accept that they'd happened. I also read that the main witness for the defence, Miss Grainne Kelly, was seriously injured and in a comma.

Although I had now regained consciousness reports were still saying I was "showing no signs of improvement". I pointed this out to mother.

"It's for your own safety," she said and I quailed, remembering Eamon.

"Eamon, where's Eamon?" I asked.

"Escaped over the border somewhere, probably Donegal," she wrote.

My look of abject terror drove her to great lengths to reassure me that he would not dare show his face in the North, but I remembered Pat's disguises and was not placated. It was then she told me about the armed guard outside my ward door. I had forgotten about the court case and poor Mick. I wore her out with questions about him. The trial had been postponed indefinitely until I was well enough to give evidence she told me.

Responsibility hit me like a fist in the guts. I could feel myself doubling up mentally against the blow. I couldn't face it any more. To give me time my mother obtained permission for me to return to Scotland for medical reasons. She had been busy on my behalf and had found a highly regarded ENT surgeon in Scotland who had agreed to look at my ears. It was now nearly five months since the accident and my hearing had not returned.

We left Altnegalvin hospital under cover of darkness and the armed guard was to remain outside my room so that it would be assumed that I was still inside. We arrived in Edinburgh airport a few hours later and headed straight for the Royal Infirmary.

It dawned on me as I looked out of the taxi at shop windows full of January Sale notices that I had missed Christmas. I mentioned this to my mum but she just shrugged her shoulders and said there would be plenty more Christmases to come. None with Patricia, I thought. Overwhelmed, I cried because I had never spent Christmas with my own child yet at the same time I knew that she would be with me every Christmas and indeed every day of my life for as long as I lived.

I was admitted to the ENT ward straight away and settled down to the prospect of spending several weeks there. A surgeon eventually operated on my right ear to remove lesions and replace the damaged eardrum with one constructed from a little bit of vein from my arm. The operation was fairly successful and I did find some hearing was returning but I was still plagued with tinnitus, and the anaesthetic had left me feeling nauseous. My stay in hospital was, therefore, prolonged.

The ward I was in was really depressing place. The other occupants were mainly elderly and suffering from ear cancer which appears to be terminal. The old soul in the bed next to me wore a towel over her head to hide her face where the cancer had broken through in a mess of stinking, weeping sores. I did my best to befriend her. And I suppose I succeeded because one night she asked me to take her to the toilet. I tried to make a joke about doing Rose Street. We would certainly have appeared drunk to the casual observer as we reeled across the ward together, her staggering because of middle ear damage and me staggering because my legs were wrecked. She managed a rye smile at my joke. Next morning she was dead.

I did make friends with a lovely woman in her mid-forties. She also had ear cancer. She also was dying. But when she got her morphine shots she was lively and talkative. From a wealthy background and well educated, she spoke like the Claire Bloom records I had once so foolishly tried to imitate. I told her the story of my image change and we had a good laugh about it. The sad thing was that she was leaving behind a son of only nine years old. When she talked about him it was always about brave or funny things he had done like the time he waded into a dog fight to save his Doberman Pincher! He had received a bite on his arm that required nine stitches, but somehow she managed to make it sound a funny story.

Other highlights of my stay in hospital were cards and visits from friends and family and letters from Emma enclosing photographs of her lovely little girl. Emma, of course, still had no idea that Patricia had ever existed or the strange cocktail of emotions that these pictures of her daughter sent spilling round my body. She sent news too of Morag who was about to get married, but I wasn't expecting an invite.

Because everybody in the ward suffered from some degree of deafness communicating was difficult. Towards the end of January we got a little Irish nurse on night duty on our ward. She was a tiny wisp of a girl with dark beautiful eyes. When she realised our difficulty, she moved our beds round in a circle with the toe ends just touching so that we could shout across to one another. We were all delighted and carried on a shouted conversation until we fell asleep. Next morning our usual dayshift dragon arrived noisier than ever, trailing the dirt of the gutter into our sterile cocoon. She charged down the ward rearranging the beds savagely to make sure everyone was awake for her morning news bulletin.

"They shot thirteen of the bastards in Londonderry last night," she announced.

"They should've shot the bloody lot!" someone said.

I leant out of bed and was sick on the floor. Nobody else in the ward seemed remotely interested.

I wanted details about the dead but all she could tell me was that they were "bloody taigs" .I told her that "taig" is the Irish name for a poet and she just snorted with derision. I finally managed to persuade an auxiliary nurse to get me a paper. The newspaper reports were frighteningly biased. Here I was in a country that I loved, amongst a people I considered friends yet, when thirteen of my fellow countrymen, British citizens like them, had been slaughtered like animals, the reports ranged from indifference to open hostility. They had their own Amritsar and they didn't see it. Ignorance is not bliss. Ignorance is the real terror. It breeds fear of our neighbours and turns friends into enemies.

I searched the list of dead and was guiltily grateful when none of them were people I knew. I was aware that they were somebody's loved ones, though, and found myself echoing my mother's phrase, "There'll be sore hearts in Derry tonight."

The attitude of the duty nurse disgusted me so much that all I wanted was to get out of that hospital and back to Derry. People there knew real suffering. I thought of the thirteen bereaved families. I thought of Patricia, Molly. Pat and Mary, young lives brutally wasted, all casualties of a political situation they had been unlucky enough to be born into, a terrible birthright that I had been shirking all my life. I thought of my mother and of Mick's parents, knew only too well that loss which is beyond the telling. Had our family not already experienced its own Bloody Sunday?

There had to be something I could do. I would start with Mick's trial. Justice for the individual might be the way forward to justice for all. It was at least worth a try. I had criminal injury money to collect, I had a decent education and I decided to put them to good use in the service of others.

I left the hospital a bent figure with a stick, looking so much older than my twenty-three years. But time was already healing my injuries and I knew I possessed a deep well of vitality from which I would be able to draw the strength and courage to walk straight and tall again. I thought of Uncle John and was determined to be a niece worthy of him at last.

I arrived in Derry to a leaden sky broken with fitful sunlight. The mass funeral of the thirteen murdered boys was taking place that day and the city was silent and exhausted. The wind flung fists of dust in my face but a great rainbow appeared for a moment over the city, softening the battle scars on the buildings and bridging the banks of the Foyle. I stood for a long time looking into the river. A flock of seabirds was a daisy patch on the soft grey lawn of the sea and, where they touched the shore the waves were writing their secrets in seaweed. I thought how the bones of the drowned lie like coral on the seabed and knew that time, like the tide, would sand my sharp bright pain as smooth and rounded as pebbles. I remembered and was grateful to the dead who are our history. Like thousands of others in Derry that day, I knelt and told them that I loved them and knew they would sleep in peace. I hoped one day to live in peace in my own country, Derry vale, beside the singing river.

d|7

Lightning Source UK Ltd.
Milton Keynes UK
25 July 2010

157432UK00002B/24/P